SHELTERING REBECCA

"When Rebecca arrives in Sally's class after being smuggled out of Germany in 1938, Sally knows little about Hitler's persecutions; but when she is given special responsibility for the young Jewish refugee, the two quickly become close friends. Working-class Sally wins a scholarship to the school that Rebecca also attends; despite class differences, the war brings the two families together in surprising ways."

—Kirkus Reviews

"Believable dialogue and smooth exposition are nicely blended. Having the story told from Sally's viewpoint gives an intimate and immediate perspective on Rebecca's problems."

—Bulletin of the Center for Children's Books

Sheltering Rebecca

Mary Baylis-White

PUFFIN BOOKS

No character in this book is intended to represent any actual person; all the incidents of the story are entirely fictional in nature.

PUFFIN BOOKS
Published by the Penguin Group
Penguin Books USA Inc., 375 Hudson Street, New York, New York 10014, U.S.A.
Penguin Books Ltd, 27 Wrights Lane, London W8 5TZ, England
Penguin Books Australia Ltd, Ringwood, Victoria, Australia
Penguin Books Canada Ltd, 10 Alcorn Avenue, Toronto, Ontario, Canada M4V 3B2
Penguin Books (N.Z.) Ltd, 182–190 Wairau Road, Auckland 10, New Zealand

Penguin Books Ltd, Registered Offices: Harmondsworth, Middlesex, England

First published in Australia under the title *Sally and Rebecca*
by Margaret Hamilton Books Pty. Ltd., 1989
First published in the United States of America by Lodestar Books, an affiliate
of Dutton Children's Books, a division of Penguin Books USA Inc., 1991
Published in Puffin Books, 1993

1 3 5 7 9 10 8 6 4 2

LIBRARY OF CONGRESS CATALOGING-IN-PUBLICATION DATA
Baylis-White, Mary.
[Sally and Rebecca]
Sheltering Rebecca / Mary Baylis-White.   p.   cm.
"First published in Australia under the title Sally and Rebecca"—
T.p. verso.
Summary: In the days before the Second World War, twelve-year-old
Sally becomes friends with Rebecca, a young Jewish refugee
from Germany.
ISBN 0-14-036448-X
[1. Friendship—Fiction.   2. Refugees—Fiction.   3. Jews—England—
Fiction.   4. World War, 1939–1945—England—Fiction.   5. Holocaust,
Jewish (1939–1945)—Fiction.]   I. Title.
PZ7.B3425Sh 1993   [Fic]—dc20   92-46592   CIP   AC
Printed in the United States of America

to my sisters,
Ruth and Anne

❖ Contents

Sheltering Rebecca

❖ Prologue: Australia Today

Clarissa was on the train alone, the first time ever without Mum or Dad or her little brother, Robert. She wriggled to the back of her seat and stared out the window at Sydney suburbs flashing past, watched as suburbs gave way to straggly bush land, and took a deep breath. In a few hours she'd be at Ulladulla with Nan and Grandpa for the holiday.

"Just me and them and my project," she told herself, shivery with excitement and a tiny bit scared.

She'd packed her swimsuit and hoped that in two whole weeks there'd be enough warm days for her to have plenty of chances to use it. The end of September and start of October were rather early in the spring season. You could never be sure, but you could always hope for the best. Thank goodness Nan wasn't a fussy grandmother.

Clarissa tore open the packet of potato chips Mum had bought her at Central Station and settled down to enjoy the journey. By the time she reached Ulladulla she'd almost finished reading her library book and had completely eaten the chips, a Crunchy Bar, and drank a can of Fanta.

And there on the platform was Nan.

They soon got over the "Haven't you grown? I'd have hardly known you." And "How's your mum and dad? And Robert?" And "You've got the spare room all to yourself this time." This last was new.

Mum and Dad always made terrible remarks about Nan's driving, and Clarissa knew why now, after sitting beside her in the front seat, rather than her usual place in the back next to Robert. But amazingly, they arrived safe and sound at Nan and Grandpa's house. They'd moved there four years ago, when Grandpa retired, so he could spend his time fishing and Nan could keep busy in a thousand different ways. Grandpa was, of course, out fishing when they arrived.

After what Nan called a wash and fresh-up they sat down to a snack of cookies and lemonade. Clarissa brought up the subject that had been on her mind ever since the last day before the holidays.

"I've got a school project to do," she said. "And I need your help."

"Fire away," said Nan, who took a big bite of ginger cookie.

"It's about our ancestors. Well, you're mine, aren't you? You and Grandpa."

"*Ancestors?*" Nan yelped and nearly choked. When she recovered, she said, "Suppose we are. Never been called an ancestor before. Makes me feel I came out of the Ark."

"I'm far too polite to make any comment," said Clarissa, mock seriously.

"Cheeky little devil." They grinned at each other. "So how am I supposed to be able to help?"

"Just by talking about your childhood to me. We're making a Grade Six book of where we all come from. Well, as far as we can. Some of us don't know. Like Janos—he's adopted. Some of us might even be descended from the first settlers. But most of us are a mixed lot, our teacher, Mr. Latimer, says. And all the better for that, he says."

"Oh, does he? Yes, you're mixed a bit, I suppose. How'd you like me to tell you about when I was your age, just before the war? Churchill's war it turned out to be, though some called it Hitler's war." Nan's face went dreamy with remembering. "It only seems like yesterday. Yes, I'll tell you about the war. And Rebecca. You should know about Rebecca."

For two weeks Nan remembered and talked. Clarissa listened and wrote most of it down. In between times, when it was warm enough, she swam.

1 ❖ New Girl: England, 1938

They were rehearsing their Christmas play when the head-master came into the classroom with a new girl.

"Back to your places," he said. "I have to talk to Miss Harrison."

"Carry on with your silent reading," Miss Harrison said.

As though anyone could. They got out their books, turned pages from time to time, between taking sneaky looks and trying to hear what was being said at the front of the room. You could hear giggles bursting out every now and then, smothered before Miss Harrison spotted the culprits. After about ten minutes of this, the headmaster left the room, and they all looked up.

"Carry on with your reading," said Miss Harrison again. "Sally Simpkins, come here a moment."

What have I done now? Sally thought, as she stood up from her desk in the back row and approached the teacher's desk.

"Sally," said Miss Harrison, "this is Rebecca Muller. She's going to be in our class and I want you to help her settle in."

Sally glanced at the new girl and gave her a welcoming smile, but Rebecca Muller just stood there staring at the floor. Was she stupid or something? Miss Harrison went on talking.

"This will be a special responsibility, Sally, and I've chosen you because I think you can handle it. You see, Rebecca has only been in England for a few weeks, and she can't speak much English yet. She's also had some very nasty experiences, so she's bound to be extra nervous at first, especially while she's learning our language."

Sally looked at Rebecca again. What sort of nasty experiences, for goodness sake? And how on earth are you supposed to help someone who can't even understand what you're saying to them?

"I'll do my best," she said, without much enthusiasm.

"I know you will. I rely on you. Take her to sit with you now."

Was that why she'd been picked? Because the other half of her double desk had been empty since Linda Schofield had left the school two weeks ago? Linda, who'd been her best friend ever since the first day in Kindergarten. "Come on," she said, and pulled the new girl along the aisle between the rows of desks.

Miss Harrison told the rest of the class some of what she'd told Sally, and forty-four heads swiveled around to have a good stare.

"Eyes to the front," Miss Harrison snapped. "Those are not the manners I expect from sixth graders."

Rebecca sat still as though she hadn't noticed everyone

looking at her. She kept her face turned down so that only the top of her head, all dark curls, showed. She sat like that for the rest of the afternoon. For once Sally was happy about the no-talking rule, but after school she felt she had to ask Rebecca what she was going to do now. She made the question as simple as she could.

"How will you get home?"

Rebecca looked at her for the first time, and Sally was startled at seeing her eyes, a strange blue with green specks in them, like a luminous watch. Over the eyes were two scowling black eyebrows.

"I do not understand."

"Come with me." Sally held her hand as she had done earlier and walked her to Miss Harrison.

"Please, Miss, how's she getting home? Is her mum coming to meet her?"

"Sally." Miss Harrison spoke in a voice barely above a whisper. "Rebecca's parents aren't here. She's staying with some other people. They'll be calling for her. You take her to the cloakroom to get your hats and coats on, then wait at the gate until they come."

"How will I know if it's the right people, and not someone kidnapping her?"

"Sally, really! You're letting your imagination run away with you. As if she'd go with anyone else except Mrs. Trevelyan. Run along now."

In the girls' cloakroom they put on their hats, coats, and gloves without talking.

"Are you a foreigner?"

"Where you from?"

Sally felt herself being jostled as four or five girls crowded around them, chattering, asking questions, giggling. Rebecca huddled against the coat pegs, looking as though she wanted to disappear through the wall.

"Shut up, and leave her alone." Sally turned on the other girls.

"Only trying to be friendly," one of them muttered back at her.

"Well leave her alone, then, like I said. Can't you see she's scared stiff with you all pushing?"

"Scaredy-cat, scaredy-cat," one of them started to chant.

"Shut up!" Sally yelled.

"Stuck up thing," one of them said.

"Teacher's pet," said another.

Sally knew it was her they were talking to now. See if she cared. They used to talk to Linda and her like that all the time, but it didn't mean anything anymore. She ignored them, and they drifted away with a few feeble jeers, leaving her alone with Rebecca.

"Mrs. Trevelyan will be at the gate, I expect," said Sally.

"Mrs. Trevelyan." Rebecca stood straighter, and her scowl eased a little.

"Come on, then." Once again Sally grabbed her hand to make sure she went in the right direction.

They were halfway down the playground when Rebecca suddenly came to life. She tugged Sally's hand, her turn to pull now, in a rush toward the gate.

"Mrs. Trevelyan!" she shouted, and waved to a woman standing there.

Sally let go of her hand and stepped back, feeling unusually shy. This Mrs. Trevelyan looked more like the lady mayoress than somebody acting as a mother. A moment later she had another shock, as Mrs. Trevelyan and Rebecca calmly climbed into a car that was parked in the street. It must have been the first time any of the children from their school had ever been taken home by car. In their town, even as late as 1938, cars were still a rarity. Only the headmaster owned one. The teachers walked or went by bus or cycled, like the children. Rebecca Muller looked like a real wonder. A foreigner, nasty experiences, and now being driven about in a car.

Sally ran all the way home. She dropped her satchel on the kitchen floor and stood with her hands pressing against her ribs, heaving to get her breath back. Jim was in his high chair; Clara and Sue, home from Kindergarten half an hour earlier, were sitting at the table. Mum sat at the other end, cutting bread and butter for their tea.

"All right, all right," said Mum. "Anyone would think there was a bogeyman after you. What's up?"

"We've got a new girl in our class." She told them about Rebecca Muller, the amazing facts she knew about her, and added, "And guess what? Miss has picked me to help her settle in."

"Quite a responsibility," said Mum. "Still, I daresay she wouldn't have chosen you if she didn't know you could be trusted. Good girl."

"That's what Miss said." No point in telling them about the empty half of her double desk, the space where Linda used to sit.

"Hey, what about our tea, Mum?" Clara said.

"Yes, I'm hungry," added Sue.

Mum set to with the bread knife again, and Sally picked up her satchel and took it up to the room she shared with Clara and Sue. Might as well start her homework now, while they were out of the way. She'd not be having her tea until Dad came home—that was the way they did it on weekdays. The three little ones first, so that Mum could get them ready for bed before Dad came home at six. Then he'd play with them and read them a story if he was in a good mood, while Mum made the second lot of tea and Sally did her homework.

Most of the kids at school didn't do homework, but she had to. This was scholarship year. Everyone in their class would take the big exams next summer, to see what school they'd go to next. She was one of the students expected to do well enough to pass to Lord George's. Every year the headmaster made the same speech when he announced the results in Assembly. She'd heard it since she was seven and knew it by heart now.

"We can't all win, but we can all have the satisfaction of knowing we've done our best. It's doing your best that's important; that's what I want to see from each and every one of you."

Then, having said all that mattered was doing your best, he'd go on and on about the great honor the scholarship winners brought to the school. It was obvious he didn't care at all about the dumb ones who'd worked as hard as they possibly could, but would never pass an exam in their lives.

The worst insult ever was to be called brainbox, so Sally wouldn't admit it, but secretly she enjoyed having to do homework. Not only because it meant she was one of the clever ones, either. She really loved quietly working on her own at English and arithmetic. She knew she'd pass the scholarship to Lord George's, and then she'd hear the second worst insult yelled at her whenever she wore her school uniform: "Lordy snob!"

Well, so what? Easy to shut your ears to that. She opened her English book and started doing that day's grammar exercise.

Two hours later she was telling Dad all about Rebecca Muller.

"She'd be a refugee, I reckon," he said.

"What's a refugee?" Sally asked him. He looked across at Mum, his face a question mark.

"Yes, it's best she should know, with things the way they are. Especially if she's got one to have to look after."

Dad took longer than usual over his next swallow of tea, then wasted more time getting out his hanky and snuffily blowing his nose. Sally felt her fingertips tingling with irritation, but she knew better than to say anything to give away her impatience. At last Dad put his hanky back into his pocket.

"We don't really know much about it," he began, "but there's this Adolf Hitler. You've heard of him?"

Sally nodded. "Sort of." What had he got to do with the new girl?

"Well, he's ruling Germany, and there are lots of people he's got no time for. Wants them out of the way. Some of them are getting out before he puts them away. Oh dear, I've not taken that much notice, but—"

"But Rebecca's only a kid! How could he even have heard of her?"

"He wouldn't have, you daft duck," Mum interrupted. "All of these people—Jews and gypsies and so on—he just wants to get rid of them. Lock, stock, and barrel."

"That's hideous." She still didn't understand but guessed that her parents didn't either. "No wonder she looked so miserable. She had a scowl on her face nearly all the time. She never smiled once."

"You'll just have to make it up to her," said Mum.

"If only she could understand what I was saying."

"She'll pick it up soon, I expect," Dad said. "Kids learn languages quicker than adults."

As she fell asleep that night Sally saw Rebecca's face in a half dream, the dark curly hair low over the scowling forehead, the blue eyes with the gleam of green saying "help me" as clearly as though she'd said the words in English.

2 ❖ Blackboard Full of Sums

How could she have missed hearing about refugees before? Now they seemed to be in the news every day. That was it, of course, they *were* news. People like Rebecca weren't safe in their own country any longer, and had to escape to places where they were foreigners. Sally tried to imagine what it must be like and couldn't. Only Rebecca's scowling face hinted at how horrible it was for her.

She didn't do the same schoolwork as everyone else. The headmaster had brought in a German-English phrase book, and told her to study that. There were written translations for her to do as well, though how anyone who didn't speak German could mark them Sally didn't know. She sneaked a look at the first pages of conversation phrases.

"Good morning. How do you do?"

"I am very well, thank you. How are you?"

"Very well, thank you. It is good weather today, isn't it?"

"Yes. But I think perhaps later we will have some rain."

Sally couldn't keep back a snort of disgust.

"Yes, Sally Simpkins? Did you want to say something?" Miss Harrison said sarcastically. Sally ignored the warning in her voice.

"It's this book of Rebecca's," she said. "It's stupid. Nobody ever talks like that."

"In the first place, you should be keeping your eyes on your own work." Miss Harrison's voice was icy. "And in the second place, perhaps you could write a better phrase book? You know all the German words, of course." A few kids sniggered.

"No, Miss," Sally muttered.

"No. Exactly. Now get on with your work without disturbing the rest of the class."

Sally was furious at the unfairness of it all, but she knew when to keep quiet. She looked at Rebecca, who returned her glance with almost a smile. Under the desk Sally stretched her leg sideways and nudged Rebecca's foot. Rebecca pressed her foot back. From that moment Sally didn't look after the new girl because she'd been told to—now they were friends.

The first Friday Rebecca was there, Miss Harrison sprang one of her spot arithmetic tests on them. There were groans all around as she started chalking up sums on the blackboard. She chuckled and went on writing numbers and arithmetical signs at top speed, enjoying her favorite joke, not shared by anyone else. Sally saw Rebecca sit up straight and look at the blackboard in surprise. As soon as Miss

Harrison turned to face them again, Rebecca waved her hand in the air like any of them did to attract attention.

"Please, Miss," she began. Everyone turned to stare at her. It was the first time most of them had heard her speak.

"Yes, Rebecca, what is it?"

"Please, Miss, I do this?"

Asking to do an arithmetic test when she didn't have to! "She must be barmy," Frank Davis whispered loudly enough for half the class to hear. He put his finger to his temple and twisted it around in the screw-loose sign. Miss Harrison pretended not to notice.

"Certainly, if you wish to, Rebecca," she said.

Rebecca looked puzzled. "Yes."

Then she relaxed and smiled. She *must* be barmy, like Frank Davis said. None of them had been able to make her smile, yet a blackboard full of sums could.

"All right, stop all this shilly-shallying," said Miss Harrison. "Get on with it now, you have exactly three-quarters of an hour."

After that the only sounds in the classroom were shuffles and sighs, the scrape and splash of pen nibs being dipped into inkwells, the scratching of pens on paper. Long before the three-quarters of an hour was over, Rebecca had finished all the sums and left her paper on top of their desk and gone back to her English phrase book.

When the papers were given back the next day she was one of the three people who'd gotten everything right, but Sally noticed that there'd been no sums that could have tricked Rebecca, like English money or weights. Was that on purpose? Must have been. So maybe Miss Harrison had her good moments after all.

* * *

Music was the next time Rebecca was especially noticed. They were in the hall, Miss Harrison at the piano, playing in her usual one-fingered fashion the melodies they were supposed to be singing. "Cherry Ripe" and "The Ash Grove" had gone their usual rollicking, not very tuneful way, with no interruptions for improvement. Music lessons were a time for everyone to let rip.

"And now let's have some Christmas cheer," said Miss Harrison. Joyously they shouted their way through "Hark the Herald Angels Sing" and "While Shepherds Watched Their Flocks by Night," without any mishaps. Only Frank Davis dared to sing the "washing their dirty socks" version of the shepherds' carol, and he changed back to the right words and a look of choirboy innocence when Miss Harrison looked up from the piano with a puzzled, suspicious frown.

She played the opening bars of "Silent Night." Sally felt Rebecca pulling her sleeve.

"I know this, we sing it in Germany. 'Stille Nacht, Heilige Nacht,' " she whispered.

Miss Harrison looked around, glaring. When she saw it was Rebecca making the noise, her one finger stopped pecking at the keyboard.

"Oh dear, perhaps you shouldn't be here. I quite forgot." Rebecca's face went blank; Miss Harrison shrugged. "We'll let it go now, shouldn't do much harm. It's not as though you know what the words mean."

"What's she going on about?" Sally whispered, but Rebecca replied with her "I don't understand" scowl. She looked as scared as she had on her first day at school, and didn't say another word all afternoon.

* * *

"It'll be because she's a Yid," Dad said that evening when Sally told him and Mum about the incident.

"A Yid?"

"Jewish, yer dad means."

"How do you know she is? You've never even met her."

"No, but she's a refugee, so she's bound to be. And they're not supposed to sing Christmas carols. Against their religion."

That still doesn't explain why she looked so scared, Sally thought.

"And while we're on the subject," Dad went on, "isn't it about time you started playing with your other friends again? You've done your job, helping her settle in. I'm all for that, but there's no need to make a meal of it."

No sense in reminding him that Linda had moved to another town, or telling him that the other girls in her class hadn't ever been all that good friends with her. He'd never understand.

3 ❖ On the Swings

The Christmas play went off as well as it usually did, with only about six catastrophes. These included one of the three kings letting his crown fall into the manger when they kneeled to worship the infant king. This might not have been too bad if only Frank Davis, who was prompting from the side of the stage, hadn't let out a really loud baby yell, "Waa, waa, waa," deliberately for the audience to hear. And in answer to the "sssshes" around him he said, in his ordinary noisy voice, "Wouldn't any baby cry if it got hit in the belly by a spiky thing like that? I'm only trying to make it realistic."

"Showing off as usual," one girl whispered, under cover of the audience's laughter. "He knows he'll get away with it because it's the end of the term."

But there was one part of the play when everyone in the audience was absolutely quiet.

The day after Rebecca had made herself noticed during

the music period, Mrs. Trevelyan had visited the head-master. A few days later Miss Harrison had sprung one of her surprises on the class.

"We're going to have some singing in the Christmas play," she told them. "We'll end up by everyone singing 'Hark the Herald Angels.' You do that jolly well, but I'd also like a solo and perhaps two or three of you together. No need to be shy. So come along, any volunteers?"

Of course there weren't.

She'd made them sing in pairs, or threes, or fours, to choose the best voices, and put Sally with Rebecca and two other girls. No words, just a tra-la-la tune she played on the piano.

The result of all this was that two boys and two girls who didn't have speaking parts in the play sang "Away in a Manger" together and Rebecca sang "Silent Night" as a solo. In German.

That was when the whole audience was quiet. She had a truly beautiful voice, and Miss Harrison didn't spoil it by playing the piano. There was just Rebecca in the center of the stage, singing on her own.

"Like a little angel, bless her," one of the mums was heard to say in a soppy voice, as the clapping at last died down.

Sally and the rest of the class had known about Rebecca's voice since the try-out day, and it had made her noticed for something else besides being foreign. But what about her being Jewish, not allowed to sing Christmas hymns? Sally knew she'd never forget the look of terror on Rebecca's face the day she'd recognized "Stille Nacht." So how, so soon, had she shed all that fear and been able to sing, as that soppy mum had said, "like a little angel"?

Rebecca's English was improving quickly, helped by Mrs. Trevelyan, who spoke German and gave her lessons most days after school. Sally asked Rebecca outright about the song.

"Yes, I am Jewish. But we did not practice the religion of the Jewish people. I have never been to synagogue, unless as a baby. I do not remember. My parents would not forbid the singing. And Mrs. Trevelyan says that here it doesn't matter that I am Jewish."

Sally remembered Dad telling her it was time she started playing with her other friends again. Playing! As if they were all seven years old. And she remembered the way he'd called Rebecca a Yid, in a funny voice, as though there were something wrong with being Jewish. All right, maybe it didn't matter to Mrs. Trevelyan, but she wasn't like most people, was she? For once Sally was pleased that she couldn't chatter to Rebecca the way she did to most people. She needed time to think.

Nobody could help where they were born, could they?

"No, here it doesn't matter," she answered Rebecca, while her mind went on whirling.

Maybe Dad had been in one of his bad moods. Maybe she'd only imagined the way he'd said those words. She hoped so.

Soon it was Christmas, and school holidays for two weeks. Grandpa came over on Christmas Day, but went home that night. Two days later, Sally went to the park by herself, to get out of having to watch Clara and Sue and Jim. She was sitting on one of the swings, ready to break her own record of how high she could go, when she heard a shout.

"Sally! Sally!"

It was Rebecca, with Mrs. Trevelyan. Sally stopped swinging to call her over, and the next minute they were seated side by side.

"I'll leave you to yourselves, then," said Mrs. Trevelyan. "I've some things to do, but I'll be back by twelve o'clock." She walked briskly to the park gates without looking back or waving good-bye to Rebecca.

They didn't talk much, just swung backward and forward, higher and higher, until they were nearly level with the top bar, squealing with fright and enjoyment. When at last they let their swings slow down, they collapsed on the wooden seats and clung to the thick metal chains, breathless and laughing. Rebecca's greenish blue eyes were brilliant, and both of their faces were bright pink in the wintry air.

Other children were crowding around, wanting turns on the swings, on the push-with-your-foot merry-go-round, and on the maypole rings.

"Phew, let's go and see the golden pheasant," Sally said.

Rebecca looked puzzled.

"It's a bird. They've got some birds in cages farther along. Come on." She grabbed Rebecca's hand to take her there. "Don't worry. We'll get back here by twelve."

"Birds. Good."

Besides the golden pheasant, there were budgerigars, finches, a peacock, and a cockatoo, in separate parts of the aviary.

"So pretty," said Rebecca. They admired the birds and talked to the cockatoo for several minutes.

"But in cages is not good," Rebecca said as they walked

away. Her eyes became moist. "I think it is time to meet Mrs. Trevelyan, yes?"

Sally looked at the watch Mum and Dad had given her for her seventh birthday, when she'd learned to tell time.

"Yes, it'll be twelve by the time we get back to the swings."

They had to wait another ten minutes for Mrs. Trevelyan. All the swings were occupied and the merry-go-rounds crowded, so they sat on a bench beneath a nearby tree. Rebecca's eyes misted up again.

"I was on a swing in a park in Germany when I said good-bye to my father," she said. "I do not think I will ever see him or my mother or my brother again. That is why I cry. I am sorry." And she started to sob.

Sally couldn't think of anything to say. She lightly patted Rebecca's arm, then held her hand. What must it be like to be in a foreign country, away from your family, maybe never to see them or any of your old friends again? It was too terrible to imagine. Sally continued to hold Rebecca's hand, and didn't try to stop her crying. All around them kids ran and played and shouted in the pale winter sunlight, taking no notice of them, thank goodness.

Maybe Mrs. Trevelyan had seen them and had waited on purpose, or it could have been sheer luck that she came up to them as Rebecca's crying was beginning to fade into shuddery breaths.

"Sorry I'm late, girls," she greeted them. "I got held up in a meeting. All set?" She said some quick words in German to Rebecca, then turned to Sally. "Can I give you a lift home? I've got the car at the gates."

"No thanks, that's all right. I'm just down the street

from the other entrance." Sally pointed to show where she meant.

"Very well, then, if you're sure. I suppose your parents will be expecting you for lunch. But what about coming around to see Rebecca this afternoon if you haven't any other plans? Does that sound like a good idea?"

Sally glanced at Rebecca, who nodded her head.

"Yes," said Sally. "Thank you," she just remembered to add.

She felt stupid, speechless, as though the lady mayoress was talking to her. Lunch. Nobody she knew had ever called dinner lunch. She'd only read it in books. They arranged to meet by the park gates nearer to where Mr. and Mrs. Trevelyan lived, at two o'clock.

4 ❖ Rebecca's Escape

Rebecca was waiting at the park gates when Sally got there. "It's not far," she said, and led the way along streets Sally had only heard about before. There was no sign of the morning's tears.

The Trevelyans' house was up a steep hill, standing by itself, with a spacious front garden and curving driveway to the front door. It seemed like a palace after the Simpkins' terrace house. Inside it was more ordinary, perhaps because, in the fading afternoon sunlight, the large rooms were as dark as those at home.

"Come to my room, please," said Rebecca. "There we can talk. Mrs. Trevelyan is busy."

Her room was wonderful. Sally gaped at the dark pink, silk eiderdown, bedspread, and matching curtains, the carpet with roses woven all over it, the huge wardrobe and the dressing table made of some dark gleaming wood, with three hinged mirrors on it.

"Look, you can see the back of your head, and half face," said Rebecca, when she noticed Sally's fascination. They spent several minutes playing with the mirrors, seeing themselves from all angles by moving them into different positions. The best fun was setting them so that they could see their reflections repeated again and again, like a long corridor going off into infinity. Sally had never seen anything like it before. She could have amused herself with those mirrors for hours.

"Thank you for letting me cry this morning," said Rebecca, when at last they finished playing mirror games. "It is the first time I have cried since I left Germany six months ago. Now I feel not so hurt inside. You understand?"

"I think so," said Sally. It was still too terrible for her to imagine.

"I will show you my family. This is the only thing I was allowed to bring when I escaped."

She opened the top drawer of the dressing table and brought out a beaded purse, the sort a young girl might carry around with her when she got dressed up. Inside it were a silver bracelet, a hand-embroidered handkerchief, and a photograph of a man, a woman, a tall boy, and a curly-haired girl, about eight or nine years old, obviously Rebecca when she was younger.

"My family. Mami, Papi, Helmut, and me." Her voice went croaky as she spoke. "I do not know what is happening to them now. I cannot write to them; it will be trouble for them. And they cannot write to me."

"But that's *terrible!*" Sally suddenly felt furious. "How can they do a thing like that? You're not criminals. Bad people," she added, when she saw Rebecca's face go puzzled, the way it did when she couldn't understand English words.

"In Germany now, to be Jewish is to be bad people. They shout at us, they break our windows, Papi cannot teach at the university, we cannot buy things in some shops . . ." Rebecca's voice faded away. The scowl she had so often came back to her face. "I must not think about it. I cannot help Mami and Papi and Helmut. Mrs. Trevelyan tells me this. I do not know."

Sally could think of nothing to say that would be of any comfort to her friend, no more than Rebecca could help her family stranded in nightmare Germany. She stretched out her hand and held Rebecca's arm gently. Rebecca took a long shuddering breath and shook her head like someone surfacing after a deep dive in a swimming pool.

"I will tell you how Mrs. Trevelyan helped me to escape," she said. "I told you I said good-bye to Papi at the swings in the park in Frankfurt. Half an hour later I left those swings with Mrs. Trevelyan. She took me across the border. She . . . what is the word for taking something from one country to another and not paying?"

"Smuggling."

"Yes, I think that is it. I had to hide under the backseat of the car. Inside the seat. She made it a place to hide. The top part was able to lift up."

Gradually, with some stumbling over words, Rebecca told the story of her flight from Nazi Germany, and the way her parents had made her leave, after her brother, Helmut, who was sixteen years old, had been taken away to the old police station one day on his way home from school.

"The police station is now Gestapo headquarters. You understand?"

Sally didn't really. *Gestapo. Nazi.* They were new words, heard more and more in the news on the wireless.

"After that day I went no more to school. Papi knew some people who helped Jews to escape. He talked to them. But only about me."

Rebecca shivered and swallowed a few times. Sally waited, her hand still on Rebecca's arm. She knew she had to keep quiet and be patient.

"Mami wouldn't leave, because of Helmut. How could she go without her son? She had to be there when the Gestapo set him free. Papi had to stop her going to their headquarters to fight them for taking her boy."

She even managed a feeble laugh as she remembered this. "Papi is so gentle and peaceful. He was loved by all his students. They were our friends before the Nazis were in power. Mami, she is different. Fighting . . . what is the word? Yes, I have it. Fierce."

But her fierce mother had agreed that if it was possible Rebecca should get out of Germany, and she had helped to coach her in the part she had to play to make this possible. Her father would go with her to a small park on the other side of Frankfurt, to avoid meeting people who knew her. There he would leave her on the second swing in the row, casually, as though they'd be seeing each other in half an hour or so. Rebecca would wear a blue ribbon in her hair for extra identification.

And, nearby, a woman on holiday from England would be sitting on a bench, enjoying a rest from sightseeing, reading a fashion magazine. She would wait twenty minutes, to make sure nobody was watching or taking special interest in her or the girl on the second swing from the left. Then she would stroll up to Rebecca and ask her, in German, if she was ready to go home for lunch. She was no longer an English woman on holiday, but a German aunt.

Rebecca was to answer yes, and hold this stranger's hand and skip along at her side, her bead purse holding her only possessions, as she began her flight to freedom.

All this had happened as planned. The English woman, who spoke such good German, had told Rebecca over and over again that this was only happening because her parents loved her and wanted her to be safe. One day, when the madness in Germany was over, they would be together again.

Near the French border, they'd stopped to eat a picnic lunch. Then came the dangerous part. Mrs. Trevelyan had chosen a quiet place away from the main road for their picnic, so that Rebecca could be hidden from the border guards in absolute safety. The trunk of her car, with its Great Britain license plates, would be opened for inspection. The chances were that no customs official would be suspicious enough to dig deeper into the car of such a respectable English lady. But they'd definitely be curious about a ten-year-old, non-English-speaking girl traveling with her.

"Later, when it was safe for me to get out, my legs were so stiff I couldn't move them. Mrs. Trevelyan had to carry me, then she rubbed my legs. It hurt a lot when they came back to life." She winced at the memory.

They traveled through France, stayed for a night at a

small hotel, and caught the channel steamer to Dover the next day. There Rebecca had her first experience of seasickness.

"And I hope it will be the last!" She shuddered and laughed.

Already she's speaking English well enough to make jokes, thought Sally. And indeed, from that day, Rebecca's English improved at an astonishing rate. It was as though the long crying session in the park had set her free to talk about her past and learn the language of her adopted country too.

The two girls met almost every day of the Christmas holidays, and slowly Sally learned about Rebecca's family, the Mullers.

She began to understand why Rebecca fit in so well with the posh Trevelyans, who still made Sally feel shy and awkward. She had to keep reminding herself of the daring risks Mrs. Trevelyan had taken to smuggle Rebecca out of Germany. That was real, as real as her grand house and upper-class accent. And anyone who risked prison or even worse at the hands of the Gestapo couldn't be too frightening, could she?

They went back to school, settled into the so-called spring term in freezing winter weather, and let their friendship grow.

5 ❖ Riverbank Accident

"Underneath the spreading chestnut tree,
Neville Chamberlain said to me,
If you want a stinking gas mask free,
Join the blooming A.R.P."

Clara and Sue were dancing about on the grass in their back garden, madly excited with the freedom of a five-week holiday from school. All the kids were singing the chestnut tree song that summer, to the tune of the old song, but with the 1939 words about England's Prime Minister, Neville Chamberlain, and the organization that worked on the Air Raid Precautions.

"Watch out!" Sally warned them. "If you bring down that washing, you'll be in trouble!"

When she wasn't at school it was her job to hang the clothes on the line on wash days, and Mum had done a huge pile today, making the most of the hot weather. She held on to the piled-high wash basket as Clara and Sue raced about, charging into her.

"Sorry, Sally," they called, and scampered on, obviously not sorry at all.

She grinned and joined in the catchy tune with her little sisters, humming it under her breath as she stretched her arms to the clothesline. Two more towels would see the end of this load, and then she'd be free to do what she liked for the next few hours. Everything's lovely, she thought, in a rush of sudden happiness. Lovely, lovely, lovely. She pushed the last clothespin down firmly, picked up the clothes prop, hooked its notched end onto the line between two double sheets, and stood it, almost upright, firmly on the grass. She waited a moment to make sure it was steady, and watched the wet clothes already blowing high above her head.

She went back into the kitchen where Mum was busy with the next load, sleeves rolled up, her arms and face bright pink from beating the heavy pounder up and down in the tub of steaming, frothy water.

"All right if I go to Rebecca's now?"

"Be back for your dinner on time, won't you?"

"Sure. Half past twelve sharp."

As Sally neared the Trevelyan house, she pulled her blouse down, making sure it was tucked securely into her Scotch kilt, and stooped to straighten her ankle socks. After more than half a year of going there, she was still in awe of Mrs. Trevelyan.

Rebecca must have heard the gate creaking, for she'd opened the front door by the time Sally was halfway up the garden path. Often they went up to Rebecca's room, but today she called back to Mrs. Trevelyan, shut the front door behind her, and came down the path to meet Sally.

"Let's stay outside in this beautiful weather, yes?"

"Yes," answered Sally. "Where shall we go?"

"The river?"

To call it a river was flattering the muddy stream, which sloshed its way across their end of the town. After a spell of dry weather, it sank down to a broad strip of sludge between banks of slimy, sickly smelling weeds. It was a little better than that today, but not much. And although it wasn't a proper river, it was at least on the edge of town where the landscape began to change to country, where it was easy to forget that they lived in part of the grimy industrial Midlands, named the Black Country because of its smoke-darkened buildings.

It was a ten-minute walk from the Trevelyans', rather more from the Simpkins', to the field path that led to the riverbank. To the left of this path was a high brick wall with bits of broken glass cemented into its top. On the right side was a hedge skirting the field. They veered to the right, ambled rather than walked, talked only now and then, plucking absentmindedly at long grasses and looking to see whether the first blackberries were ripe yet. They weren't.

As they sauntered along the path, which twisted with the turns of the river, they wondered what it would be like at Lord George's after the holiday. Rebecca hadn't taken the scholarship. Mrs. Trevelyan had arranged for her to go as a private pupil.

"I bet you'd have even passed the English exam if they had let you do the tests," Sally assured her. "And you'd have beaten everyone in arithmetic."

"Not with all those yards, feet, and inches, and pounds, shillings, and pence, I wouldn't," said Rebecca. "Thank goodness the Trevelyans can afford to pay the fees, though."

"Yes. And thank goodness I passed, so we won't be split up. What the . . . ?"

The last words were a yelp as they leaped to dodge out of the way of three bicycles racing around a curve, taking up the whole width of the path. Rebecca jumped to the left and slithered down the shallow bank into slimy weeds and mud. Sally landed half in the hedge, one of her feet entangled in the spokes of the front wheel of the bike nearest to her.

"Ouch!" she cried, as she tried to free herself. "Why don't you watch where you're going?"

"Why don't you? We've got as much right here as you have," said the biggest boy. At his words the other two, who'd looked a bit bothered, changed their attitudes.

"Yeah, bloody girls, think you can take up all the path."

"Come on, it's not worth a fight," said the third one. "This wheel'd better not be damaged, that's all."

They cycled off.

"Good riddance to bad rubbish," Sally yelled after them. "Ouch."

She sat down on the path to pick thorns and leaves off her blouse, not looking at what she was doing, gazing instead at the foot that had been caught in the bike wheel. Then she looked down to the riverbed and forgot her injured foot.

"Rebecca!"

Rebecca was huddled, half in the river slime, whimpering like a frightened animal, her whole body shaking.

"Rebecca!" Sally called again, more softly. "It's all right."

Rebecca's face was ghastly when at last she looked up, pale with terrible staring eyes. "Have they gone?" she whispered.

"Yes," Sally assured her. "And they won't be back. Don't worry. Look, they're only ordinary stupid boys." Rebecca still huddled, trembling. "They're not Hitler Youth!" Sally shouted.

It was cruel, meant to shock. Cruel to be kind, Sally reasoned, and it worked.

Rebecca shuddered, made a noise between a gasp and a scream, and put her hands over her mouth. After a minute or so she stopped shaking.

"I'm sorry," she said.

"Don't be sorry. You have nothing to be sorry for. It's what happened to you; those other people in Germany, they should be the ones who are sorry." She let her voice fade away; there was no point in saying any more about it. It wouldn't help.

Rebecca scrabbled about in the mud, looking for hand-and footholds to climb up to the path. Sally moved forward to give her a hand up and was stopped by a fierce twinge in her left foot, shooting all the way up her leg. She couldn't restrain a yelp of pain. Rebecca slithered back into the slime, cowering.

"It's all *right*, those boys aren't coming back," Sally told her, wincing again, impatient despite her sympathy for Rebecca's past.

"So why do you shout like that?" Rebecca's voice was suspicious with fear.

"Because of my foot, that's why. It hurts like mad."

"Oh, I am so selfish. You're hurt." Rebecca clambered up onto the path, her own fear vanishing in concern for her friend.

"Just look at you," Sally said, "and phew, you really stink!" She wrinkled her nose, made a face, and broke their somber mood. They both giggled, half hysterically.

Rebecca was a repulsive sight and smell, half covered with slime from the riverbed.

"What will Mrs. Trevelyan say when she sees you like that?"

"I think she will laugh. I hope so."

Laugh! Sally could just imagine what Mum would say if *she* walked in looking like that, and especially on washing day. Must be lovely to have a washerwoman. For a moment she envied Rebecca, forgetting her horrific tragedy.

"What about your foot? Do you think it's broken?"

"I don't know. I'll rest it a bit and see if the pain wears off. Look behind us."

"Where?" Rebecca looked up and down the path, as though she were still scared the boys might return.

"No, not there. In the hedge. Here." Sally wriggled back, sitting down, to pull apart the hedge where she'd fallen through.

The ground sloped up steeply, so that the other side of the hedge was level with the tops of Rebecca's legs as she stood and peered through the space Sally had made. Rebecca gasped.

"Yes, you'd never guess it, would you?"

Sally pulled herself up until she was standing, careful not to put any weight on her injured foot.

* * *

They stood side by side looking into the grottolike space made by the hedge on their side and another hedge bordering a field. Two hedges, starting and finishing together, one straight, one curved, to make the field edge tidy, to flatten the bulge on the river path. The space between the hedges was the size of a very large cupboard or a very small room, shaped rather like a new moon. Nobody walking along the field or the river path would guess it was there. They looked at each other with the joy of discovery. No need to say anything—both knew that this would be their own secret place for the summer holiday.

"Now we must go home," said Rebecca. "For your foot."

"I suppose so."

"How can I help you?"

"Like this."

She put her arm across Rebecca's shoulders to use her as a human crutch. It took much longer than the usual ten minutes to reach the Trevelyans' house, and by the time they were there Sally knew she would never be able to walk the extra distance home on her own.

Rebecca used the brass lion's head door knocker instead of going to the unlocked back door as they normally did. Their plight warranted a more formal entry. Mrs. Trevelyan opened the door, and at the sight of the two bedraggled creatures took a step backward.

"What on earth have you done to yourselves?"

She led the way along the hall and into the kitchen without waiting for their reply.

"Some boys on bicycles knocked us over. I fell in the river."

"River!"

"It wasn't deep," Sally said quickly, "mud mostly."

"Quite." Mrs. Trevelyan wrinkled her nose, and they all laughed. "You'd better get out of those clothes straight away. And have a hot bath."

Rebecca didn't need to be told twice.

Sally always felt nervous if she was left alone with Mrs. Trevelyan, even for a minute. Now she had to go through this ordeal for as long as Rebecca took to have a bath and change into clean clothes. Oh, help! A stab of pain in her foot made her forget this lesser worry.

"Let's have a look at your injury," Mrs. Trevelyan said. Sally sat on a kitchen chair with her foot propped on a stool. The bar of her sandal was cutting across her instep and her foot was beginning to swell ominously.

"We'd better have your sandal off. Do you want to do it or shall I?"

"I'll do it," said Sally. It hurt worse than ever as she undid the buckle. She couldn't bear the thought of pulling her ankle sock over that great swollen lump.

"Leave your sock on—it'll act as a support. But I'll get a bandage as well."

"There," she said a few minutes later, "how does that feel?"

"Much better, thank you." It really did.

"Good. But you'll have to see a doctor. This is only temporary first aid. Would you like me to ring mine now?"

"Please don't. Mum can get ours."

"All right, I suppose that makes sense."

Sally breathed a sigh of relief.

"But you can't possibly walk home in that state. As soon as Rebecca's out of the bath I'll drive you home." Sally just sat there. How could she object? There was a minute or two of silence.

"Tell me, Sally, how do you think Rebecca's settled in? You know her better than anyone here."

Sally was saved from answering when Rebecca returned, looking fresh and bright in a clean dress.

"We'd better get you back to your family. Come along, Rebecca, we'll carry her between us," said Mrs. Trevelyan.

She had to show Rebecca how to link their hands into a firm seat. Sally edged onto this, her arms across their shoulders, and they carried her out to the garage.

6 ❖ The Hole in the Hedge

All the way back in the car Sally worried about how she could keep them out of her house. She'd never taken Rebecca inside, and washing day would be the worst possible time to introduce her to everyone. She didn't know what Clara and Sue would be up to, and more likely than not Jim would be running about half naked, with the wrong half showing. Since he'd been out of diapers, he'd taken to stripping off his underpants and trousers too. Mum had given up trying to keep him decent except when they went out. Mum would have a fit if she walked in with Rebecca and Mrs. Trevelyan.

"I'll be able to manage by myself now," Sally said as the car slowed down outside their house.

"Are you sure?"

"Sure, thanks. And thank you for the first aid and ride home." Any other time such luxury would have been the thrill of the century.

"That's the least we could do. Well, if you're certain you'll be all right, we'll be getting back. Be sure to let us know what the doctor says, won't you?"

"Yes, I will. Thank you."

Sally climbed out of the car, hopped across the pavement, and up the path to the back door.

"You're back early," Mum greeted her. "Oh my Gawd, what have you done?"

Sally told her about the mad boy cyclists, about how Mrs. Trevelyan had bandaged her foot and said she'd have to see a doctor.

"Oh, she said you'd have to see a doctor, did she?" Mum's voice was furious. "I'll decide that for myself, thank her ladyship very much. Here, let's have a look at it."

Clara and Sue came rushing into the kitchen from outside.

"What's happened?" Clara asked, puffing after her run down the street.

"Why did you come home in a car?" Sue made it sound like a royal coach. "Ooooh!" She'd just seen Sally's bandaged foot.

Her sisters watched Mum unwind the bandage and peel off the sock. Sally's eyes filled with tears of pain as the top of her sock was stretched to go over her heel. But the next minute she decided it was worth it, to see her ankle, swollen like a half-blown-up balloon, already a fascinating shade of purple. Clara and Sue were so awed by the sight that they didn't even speak.

"Yes," Mum admitted, "we'll certainly need to have that looked at. I'll go and call the doctor right away."

They'd had the phone in the house less than a year. Nobody had started using it casually yet.

"Doctor said to keep it rested for now, he'll be here as soon as he can," Mum reported back. "You'd better go and lie down on the settee."

Sally hopped through the kitchen and dining room, across the hall, and into the front room. "Get me my library book, will you?" she asked Clara. "You know, the Angela Thirkell one." Clara went upstairs without a word of protest. Wonderful what a dramatic injury could do.

The doctor pressed and turned and kneaded her ankle so much she had to bite her lips to stop herself from yelling out loud. He decided there were no bones broken.

"But you've got a nasty sprain there, young lady," he said. He bound it up and gave Mum orders about cold compresses and changing the bandages. "Keep off it for a couple of days, but don't leave it too long. Try walking on it on Wednesday. See how it goes." He turned to Mum. "Just let her do it in gradual stages. Give me a ring if it doesn't seem to improve. There shouldn't be any problems, though. She's a healthy lass. I think we can let nature take its course."

The weather changed to dull and cloudy, with odd drizzles of rain, so Sally quite enjoyed the next two and a half days. The novelty of being her fetching-and-carrying slaves soon wore off for Clara and Sue, but she wanted to be alone to wallow in the luxury of uninterrupted reading, anyway. Mum had gotten her another school story and two funny books from the library first thing on Tuesday morning, so she was able to lie on the settee, "like Lady Muck," as Dad said when he got home from work that day.

* * *

The swelling went down, and the bruises faded with surprising speed, so that less than a week later Sally was able to go out and see Rebecca again.

"And remember," Mum called to her as Sally went out the back door, "no doing anything daft to hurt it again."

"Of course not. It wasn't my fault before."

Rebecca met her at the Trevelyans' gate.

"I've been back to that hole in the hedge," she said. "It's perfect. Nobody would see us and the ground's dry. Being high the rain must drain off to the river path."

It was easy to wriggle through the hedge. The only difficult part for Sally was clambering up the rise from the path with her ankle still not completely healed. The top of the hedges spread into an overhang, and a tree on the side by the field made a wider shelter still, giving the area a full leafy roof. It was cozy, mysterious, magical.

"Yes, you're right," said Sally. "It's absolutely perfect."

Trembling with spooky excitement, they sat down on the hard ground, lumpy with surface roots and fallen twigs. From a sitting position, their heads were about level with the heads of people walking along the riverbank. It was weird to hear snatches of conversation. Several times they had to cover their mouths to stop giggling out loud.

But they weren't there to eavesdrop; neither did they plan to use this place to hide anything except themselves. It wasn't all that likely that anyone else would discover it as they had, but it could happen. During the last few months they'd spent many hours in Rebecca's room. Mrs. Trevelyan left them alone, so they were sure of privacy there, but an outdoor place that nobody else knew about had an extra enchantment. In the dark green hole between the hedges it was easy to pretend that the outside world didn't exist. Everywhere else it was getting more and more difficult to ignore what was happening in that outside world.

War. War. War. All that summer holiday it was coming closer. When they were together Sally and Rebecca hardly ever mentioned it. Sally tried to convince herself that she was protecting Rebecca by not reminding her of the terrible times she'd had in Germany, or of her parents and brother still left there. Really she knew that she didn't dare think about it herself. So she chattered on about going to high school, about her brother and sisters, anything except war. Rebecca chattered back, and they both laughed loudly at feeble jokes. They spent as much time as they could in the hole in the hedge, safe in their secret place.

Outside, people weren't saying, "if there's a war," any longer. Now they were saying, "when the war comes." Anderson shelters were springing up in back gardens like so many corrugated-iron igloos; empty shops were being converted into air-raid wardens' posts; and kids like Clara and Sue could be heard singing the spreading chestnut tree song in every street.

You didn't have to join the blooming A.R.P. to get your stinking gas mask free, though. They were giving them away to everyone. The day the Simpkinses got theirs, Dad made the entire family practice putting them on properly.

"Oh help, do we have to?" Clara whined.

"Yes, this could save your lives," Dad said. Clara and Sue made faces at each other, behind Dad's back. Sally felt sick with fear.

She felt sick at the hot rubbery smell, too, like having gas at the dentist's. Mum had to fetch Jim from the garden to have his mask fitted on. He came in with her easily enough, then saw his big sisters looking like monsters from a nightmare and screamed louder than they'd ever heard him scream before. Mum grabbed him as he made a dive for the open doorway. He yelled louder still, trying to pull her outside as well. Sally quickly undid her mask and took it off.

"Look, Jim, it's only me," she said. "See? We're just playing a funny game."

She signaled to Clara and Sue to take their masks off too, and they were only too happy to obey her. Jim still clung to Mum, his head pushed into her apron, his feet clattering on the floor in a frenzy to get away. They all spoke to him to let him know it was them, that he was safe, but it took quite a time to calm him down enough for his cries to fade to gulps and sobs.

"What if we have to wear them really, if there's a gas attack?" Clara asked. "He'd be killed if he didn't wear his." At this, Sue looked as though she was going to cry too.

"We'll worry about that when it happens," said Dad. "With a bit of luck we won't need to wear them at all."

War or no war, they still had to get Sally ready for Lord George's. She and Mum went, with the printed list they had from the school, to the shop in town that sold the uniforms.

"They even tell you how many pairs of knickers to buy, and what sort. Gosh!" They looked at each other, snorting with laughter. The shopping spree became a hilarious outing.

"Hey, shurrup," Mum said, between laughs. "The shop

girls'll think we're crackers." But the funny side of it stopped her from worrying about all the money they were being forced to spend.

After that, Sally spent every wet day sewing Cash's name tapes onto garment after garment, onto her shoe bag and canvas shoes, and finally onto her handkerchiefs. Everything would be ready in September when the new school year started.

The Simpkinses were sitting at breakfast on Friday, September 1, when they heard on the wireless the news that the German army had invaded Poland.

"That's it, then," said Dad.

"Yes," said Mum. "Oh, good Lord, whatever shall we do?"

"We can only carry on as normal, ducks. I'll have to be off to work, no sense in losing pay for being late. Ring me at the works if I'm needed, eh?"

"Right you are."

It was horrible to see Mum and Dad scared. They were covering it up as well as they could, but Sally wasn't fooled by their casual words. And if they're scared, who is there to look after us, she thought. She rushed to finish making her bed and washing the dishes, with Clara and Sue drying. The sooner she could escape to the hole in the hedge the better.

"I'm just going around to Rebecca's," she told Mum.

"I'd rather you didn't, today."

"Why?"

"You'd be better off at home. There's no knowing what's going to happen."

"Look. Even if the war started now, this very minute,

❖ 44 ❖

bombs aren't going to come dropping out of the sky onto me straight away, are they?"

Mum frowned while Sally went on arguing, until Jim caused a diversion by yelling in another room. Mum looked weary as she automatically went to see what was the matter with him.

"All right," she said. "But be sure you're back in good time for your dinner."

"Of course, Mum. And try not to worry."

She had a sudden desire to put her arms around Mum and hug her, but such unusual behavior would certainly have given her something to really worry about. Sally restrained the impulse.

7 ❖ "It's Too Late Now"

Rebecca and the Trevelyans heard the news of the invasion of Poland while they were eating their breakfast, too. Paul Trevelyan, like Ken Simpkins, hesitated about whether to go to work that day and decided he ought to. He wouldn't lose any pay if he was late, or even if he took the whole day off, because the factory he went to, in that Midland town crowded with small factories, was his own.

"It would look bad to the men and women if I didn't show up as usual," he said.

He'd not been gone long before Sally arrived. Mrs. Trevelyan answered her knock on the back door and spoke to her in a whisper.

"Come in. I'd like a few words with you before you go up to Rebecca."

Sally noticed that the door from the kitchen out to the

hallway was shut. She couldn't remember ever seeing it closed before.

"Rebecca's going through hell today, as you can imagine," said Mrs. Trevelyan. "I'm sure she'll want to see you later, but at the moment I think she wants to be on her own. She's crying and she shut her door very firmly."

Sally remembered the day in the park all those months back when she'd first seen Rebecca cry. What an age away that seemed now. The day when suddenly Mrs. Trevelyan was someone she could talk to like an ordinary person, not somebody to be scared of. Slowly since then she'd been able to see Mrs. Trevelyan growing more real, and not only because her name was in the local paper almost every week. She was famous for her "good works," but that didn't help Sally to feel easier in her company. On the contrary. No, it was the way Rebecca talked about her, so casually, and as Celia now, not as Mrs. Trevelyan. Mr. Trevelyan was Paul, too. Sally had only seen him twice. Then the day she sprained her ankle, a few weeks back, had been the start of really feeling at ease with Mrs. Trevelyan.

"How about some lemonade and cookies?"

"Thanks, Mrs. Trev . . ." How could she be callous enough to eat and drink when her best friend was suffering so much? She stopped in horror at herself. "Trevelyan," she finished, after a pause.

"I rather like 'Mrs. Trev,' as you can't bring yourself to call me Celia." So Mrs. Trev she was from then on.

While Sally ate the cookies and drank the lemonade, Mrs. Trev talked about the plight of other refugees she had helped to rescue, and those German Jews she had not been able to rescue.

"That horrible regime. God alone knows what will happen now." She banged her fists on her forehead, then looked across at Sally. "I'm sorry. I shouldn't be burdening you with all this. You're only a child." There was no trace of the grand lady in the face Mrs. Trev turned to Sally. It was the face of one desperate human being looking to another for help.

"I'll tell Rebecca you're here. All right?"

"Yes."

Mrs. Trev went out of the kitchen, this time leaving the door open. Sally heard her go upstairs, heard her knock on Rebecca's door, heard that door open and close, then silence. She drank more lemonade and ate another cookie while she waited. She felt as though she grew up ten years in those ten minutes.

Mrs. Trev called her from upstairs. Sally and Mrs. Trev met outside Rebecca's room and didn't say a word, only exchanged looks and nods and a quick clasp of hands.

Rebecca was sitting on the edge of her bed, hunched over, holding the photo of the Muller family in one hand, her other hand pulling at the threads of the dark pink bedspread. She looked up as Sally walked into the room, and gazed at her as if she were a stranger. Recognition came to her eyes.

"It's too late now, it's too late," she cried over and over again. Sally sat beside her on the bed and put her arm across her friend's shaking shoulders. She didn't need to ask what was too late. Mrs. Trev's mention of those Jews who hadn't escaped, whom she hadn't been able to help, gave her the answer. The last doors of escape had clanged shut with Hitler's invasion of Poland and the near certainty of war between England and Germany.

"Until today I suppose I always hoped, deep down, that they'd get out. Now I know they never will." She slumped forward again, her shoulders drooped, but they weren't shaking anymore.

Sally looked at her watch surreptitiously. Twenty-five past twelve! Mum would be expecting her home in five minutes, and she'd never make it, even if she ran every step of the way. In any case, how could she possibly leave Rebecca now? She must stay with her, at least for the next few hours. How to arrange this without looking as though she was sponging a meal?

Mrs. Trev's perfect timing saved her from having to work this out. At that very moment there was a knock on the door and a call of "May I come in, girls?"

"Yes, of course," they answered together.

"Sally, you must stay for lunch. You will, won't you?"

"If Mum'll let me. Can I phone her?"

"Certainly. You know where the phone is, in the hall. Go along, I'll stay here with Rebecca."

Mum started off being argumentative, then cringing about accepting charity.

"*Mum!* It's me who's helping them by staying. Can't you understand? Rebecca needs me here today. And so does Mrs. Trevelyan." She would never be Mrs. Trev to Mum.

"Well, if you're sure."

"I'm sure."

"And remember to thank Mrs. Trevelyan."

"*Mum!*"

* * *

Mrs. Trev had made them a plate of sandwiches, some egg, some watercress, some tomato. Sally tried not to look too greedy, but she felt ravenous. Rebecca just nibbled at one watercress sandwich all the way through the first part of that midday meal. Sally deliberately lost count of the sandwiches she ate, followed by a piled-up dish of stewed blackberries and apple with real cream. At least Rebecca ate that as though she knew what she was doing.

"I think we need some music," said Mrs. Trev, after they'd finished the last mouthfuls of blackberry and apple.

Although Sally had been to the Trevelyans' house many times, it was the first time she'd been in their living room. She'd thought Rebecca's room was luxurious, but it was nothing compared to this—carpet that your feet sank into, a long settee and four armchairs all covered in gold velvet, small carved tables here and there, and by one wall, a grand piano.

Mrs. Trev played the sort of music on this piano that Sally had heard only on the wireless. She didn't quite know what to make of it, especially the bits that had no real tunes. Some parts were lovely, though, and Sally saw the tight look on Rebecca's face soften as Mrs. Trev played. She finished with a quick, jolly piece that made them all smile.

"All right, Rebecca, your turn," Mrs. Trev said. It was an invitation, not a command. Sally decided that Rebecca's playing was . . . well . . . interesting. She played some simple pieces with obvious enjoyment, and made a lot of mistakes and stumbles when she tried something more difficult.

"I should stick to singing," she apologized, with a feeble laugh. That laugh was the best music Sally had heard all afternoon. Before lunch she wouldn't have thought Rebecca could ever laugh again.

"Do you play the piano, Sally?" Mrs. Trev asked her.

"Only 'Chopsticks' and 'Oh, Can You Wash Your Father's Shirt?,' and I'm not playing either of them after real music."

The laughter all three of them shared was that of sheer good-humored friendship.

8 ❖ Peace on Earth

"Will you be called up?" Sally asked Dad, as soon as they'd heard Neville Chamberlain announcing the start of the war on that frightening Sunday morning, September 3, 1939.

"Not yet, at any rate. They'll have the under-forties first."

"Aye, and they'll want to keep you out, too," said Mum. "They can't take fellers with four kids to look after, surely."

Dad roared with laughter. "I'd like to see them counting kids. Be a funny sort of war if we let you women run it."

"If it was up to the women there wouldn't be any war," Mum retaliated. "Nor no Hitler, neither. We'd have soon put an end to him. I'm going to make a pot of tea."

During the next few weeks Sally wondered what they'd all been so scared of. Being at war was hardly any different from peacetime. No air raids, no drama. Just the heavy blackout shades to put up every night, the quiet, dark streets if you peeped under those heavy window blinds, and having to remember to carry your gas mask everywhere you went. Sally and Rebecca had taken these to their secret place by the river and played spooky games with them, but with war almost there, and high school too, they had suddenly seemed to have grown away from its magic.

Starting high school was much more of an ordeal. On the first morning, self-conscious in their new uniforms, Sally and Rebecca met at a street corner they both had to pass on their way. Thank goodness they had each other for support. Three prefects stood at the school gate, holding lists of names and checking off all the new girls as they walked in. "Go into the inside playground," they said, pointing to a huge, barnlike room with bare brick walls and a stone floor. In this bleak place, ninety new girls stood about in attitudes ranging from bravura to undisguised nervousness, until the prefects at the gate joined them. Reading their lists aloud, they divided the girls into Upper III a, b, and c. Sally and Rebecca curled their little fingers together until both their names had been read out. Both were in the same form, thank goodness, in Upper IIIa.

The school was three stories high, above a maze of basement for cloakrooms, storerooms, and kitchens. Every story extended out in two or three directions, and there were staircases all over the place, with long, straight corridors connecting them. "Follow me, Upper IIIa," said one of the prefects, and thirty girls straggled after her.

"We'll never find our way around this maze," grumbled one of the bolder girls.

"You'll be surprised," the prefect said. "But remember, no noise in the corridors. The rest of the school's begun first period." There were a few smothered giggles at that, silenced as they reached their form room and were introduced to their form mistress.

"You'll sit in alphabetical order, starting here, Josie Anderson. Go to your desks as I say your names. And answer your name, so that we can leave places for anyone who's absent."

Sally and Rebecca looked regretfully at each other as they sat in their widely separated seats. Never mind, they'd be together at playtime. No, recreation, they'd have to learn to call it. At Lord George's, everything had different names.

"And remember that I have a surname, which I expect you to use. My name is not 'Miss.' Girls who were at elementary schools will have to remember that. Of course, you girls who were at our junior school know that already." She gave a thin-lipped smile. "Now, copy out the timetable." This filled the large blackboard and was a mass of letters and numbers that made hardly any sense, except for the more recognizable subject names such as English and history.

By the end of the school day, Sally's head felt as though it were full of wasps. She'd never sort it all out. While they had their tea, she told the rest of the family how confusing the day had been.

"You'll get used to it," said Mum.

"That's what everyone says. I bet I never will. And another thing, nobody thinks you're good because you passed the scholarship. They keep saying, 'you scholarship girls' and 'you girls from the elementary schools,' as if we came from pigsties or something."

"What did I tell you? I always said her winning that scholarship would do us no good," Dad muttered.

"Get off," Mum answered him. "She'll be as right as rain in no time, you'll see. In any case, there's nothing we can do about it now, so just get on with your tea."

Mum was right. In a surprisingly short time Sally felt as though she'd been at Lord George's all her life.

Air-raid practices were the highlight of that first term. The shelters were scattered about the playground. There was a complicated system of which shelter you went to, according to the room you were in when the warning bell rang. As they changed rooms every period, the girls had to carry charts around with them, as well as their books, pens, pencils, rulers, rubbers, gas masks, and gym things—not to mention such extras as geometry sets and botany samples. They usually spent about twenty minutes down in the shelters while the mistress in charge of each form called the roll, and Miss Mirvine, the headmistress, went on her rounds, from shelter to shelter, to ensure that everyone was in her right place.

"As if she'd do that in a real air raid," said Sally to Rebecca.

"Exactly. She wouldn't risk being blown up by a bomb just to see that we were all in our right and proper places."

But they weren't complaining. Shelter practice was fun, a welcome break in the routine.

By Christmas there still hadn't been any real air raids and school had become ordinary. As soon as the holidays began, the Simpkinses started to get ready for Grandpa's visit. Mum had tried to persuade him to stay for the whole of their time off from school, but he'd stubbornly said he'd be there only for Christmas week. "I'll come on Monday and go back Friday," he insisted. "That way I won't miss the Sunday services."

"Anyone would think the choir would go dumb without him," said Mum.

Sally, Clara, and Sue all went to meet him at the bus stop. Clara and Sue jumped up and down with excitement as they waited, keeping warm as well. Sally would have done the same if she hadn't felt she was too old for such behavior in public. Two Midland Red buses stopped. A few people got off each time, and others got on for the last stage of the journey into the town center. The third bus was the one they were waiting for. First a woman with two loaded shopping bags stepped off, then Grandpa, white-haired and as rosy-cheeked as Santa Claus.

Clara and Sue greeted him with cries of "Grandpa! Grandpa!" and leaped up to kiss him. Sally gave him a hug and a kiss, too, as soon as she had the chance.

"What a welcome! And bless my soul, how you've all grown."

"I'm eight now, and Sue's six and a half," said Clara quickly.

"Goodness me. Well I never, what big girls. And you must be eleven, Sally, eh?"

"That's right, Grandpa." She linked her arm in his as they set off on the walk home. All the way Clara and Sue vied with each other to tell him everything that had happened since his last visit. They skipped along backward, facing Sally and Grandpa, talking over the top of each other, hardly stopping for breath. Grandpa gave Sally's hand a squeeze with his arm, and she smiled at him, sharing his amusement. She felt warm with the happiness of the moment.

"I've put you in with Jim, Dad," Mum told Grandpa when they arrived at home. "He never wakes in the night now."

"Don't talk too soon," Sally warned her. "You're tempting fate."

The next day, Christmas Eve, the three young ones were in such a state of excitement that the rest of the family was more exhausted at their bedtime than they were.

"I still don't see," said Clara, "how Santa Claus is going to do his rounds tonight with the searchlights and barrage balloons and all that."

"I told you," Sally said, "it's all part of the magic."

Clara eyed her skeptically.

"I'm not going to tell you once more," Mum threatened. "Christmas or no Christmas, it's time you were in bed. Go on, this minute."

The youngsters scuttled off upstairs, and when Mum and Dad had at last tucked them in, Sally, Grandpa, Mum, and Dad started filling stockings. It was the first time Sally had been allowed to help with this, and she found it was even more fun than wondering what she was going to get herself. She kept imagining the little ones' faces in the morning. At the best of times, the Simpkinses had never had much in the way of presents. This Christmas, with rationing, Mum had needed to use a lot of ingenuity, but had managed to find small surprises for everyone.

"Mabel," Grandpa said to her as they sat by the fire when the work was finished, "I'd like to go to the Christmas service tomorrow. The Baptist chapel's got one at eleven—I looked it up in your local paper. It won't put you out if I go, will it?"

"Of course not, Dad. I'd join you, to keep you company, only with the dinner to cook . . ." She shrugged her shoulders.

"I'd like to go with you, Grandpa," said Sally on a sudden impulse.

"Hey, not so fast," said Dad. "What about giving your mother a hand in the kitchen? Christmas dinners don't cook themselves, you know."

"No," Mum agreed, "and it's not every day Sally wants to go to church with her grandpa, either. So seeing as how you're so worried about me slaving away in the kitchen you can do your fair share."

"Well, I'll be . . ." Dad scratched his head, but he knew when he was beaten.

What had made her say she wanted to go to church for the Christmas service? She didn't know, except it wasn't only because she wanted to be with Grandpa. It had something to do with the confused thoughts she'd had about religion since she'd known Rebecca. She was a refugee simply because she was born a Jew, even though her family didn't practice the Jewish faith. And what if they had? Why should people be persecuted because of their race or religion? It didn't make sense. The Simpkinses didn't practice any sort of Christian faith, and they'd stopped going to Sunday School when Jim was born, because it had been too much bother for Mum to get them all ready.

The next day she didn't think about this, and it just felt good to walk right over to the other side of town with

Grandpa, wearing the new red scarf and gloves Mum and Dad had given her.

The chapel was almost full. The minister spoke, as thousands of priests, bishops, curates, and clergy of all denominations spoke that day, about peace on earth and goodwill toward men. England was a country at war, although it didn't seem like it. There'd been no bombings yet; nobody in that chapel had lost a son or a husband or a brother.

The congregation cheerfully sang the well-known carols, Grandpa's strong bass voice, his secret vanity, harmonizing perfectly with the melody sung by most of the people. Sally joined in the singing, filled with a rare emotion she recognized as pure joy. It was a wonderful experience, something to hold onto, a memory to cherish. For those minutes in the church the war was forgotten. It really felt as though there was peace on earth.

9 ❖ The Morrison Shelter

The hymn in morning assembly had been "For All the Saints," the duty prefect had read the first seven verses of the second epistle to the Corinthians, and Miss Mirvine had prayed for comfort to the bereaved. At the final "amen" the girls waited for the usual signal to sit down, but Miss Mirvine stood still, gazed over the six hundred heads, and said quietly, "Please remain standing." All over the hall girls in their rows glanced at neighbors with raised eyebrows, shrugging their shoulders.

It was the end of the first week in June, 1940, later to be called Dunkirk week. Newspapers had been full of stories of fishermen, seamen, men in boats of all sizes who had risked their lives to rescue fellow countrymen. Faces everywhere glowed with glory, as though some great victory had been won. Miss Mirvine's face showed no glory.

"Today I have to tell you of the tragedy that has befallen a member of this school. Yesterday evening the parents of Marion Oldham, from Upper IVb, heard that their only son, Keith, serving in His Majesty's army, lost his life on the shores of France during the evacuation from Dunkirk. Will you please bow your heads in silent prayer for Keith, and ask for God's comfort to his family and to all those who grieve for loved ones who have lost their lives in these perilous times.''

Sally heard Rebecca make a sound that could have been a gasp or a sob. She didn't look at her, but gave her a quick nudge of sympathy. She'd have held her hand, but one of the prefects on duty at the sides of the hall would be sure to notice, and then they'd both be in trouble. No sense in adding an irritating school upset to Rebecca's real tragedy.

All the rest of the day Rebecca was quiet, her face scowling, her eyes dull, in the way Sally had seen her so many times—the times when she was remembering her family.

So Sally was all the more surprised the next day to see Rebecca's greenish blue eyes brilliant with life again.

"Can you come around to my house after school?" Rebecca asked her.

"Sure. I'll phone Mum from there if that's all right."

"Of course."

"What's it all about?"

"Wait and see."

On the long walk home Rebecca told her a little more. "Celia's making us an air-raid shelter."

"Building you one?" Mrs. Trev was full of surprises.

"No!" Rebecca laughed. "She's making the cellar into one."

Sally had been to the cellar once, when they hadn't known what to do on a rainy Saturday and Rebecca had suggested they explore there. It was as wide and long as the whole house, large enough for a family to live in comfortably. Coal was stored at one end, in a bricked-off section; farther along the same end was a part used as a workshop, with an adjoining bathroom complete with bath, hand basin, and lavatory; at the other end, Paul Trevelyan had fitted a few wine racks. The large space in between each end was mostly filled with junk, scattered about.

Now the junk and cobwebs were cleared away, and the concrete floor was swept and covered with raffia matting.

"Mrs. Trev did all this in one day?"

"Not on her own. Mrs. Brown did the physical work, of course. And we all helped to put down the matting."

Sally could never get used to the idea that the Trevelyans had a "daily woman" to do their housework.

During the next few days the cellar was equipped with three folding beds and blankets, and the shelves were stocked with precious tinned foods bought before rationing. Mrs. Trev had even managed to find a portable stove.

"You are lucky," said Sally, and she could have bitten her tongue out. "Sorry, but you know what I mean."

"Yes, and I agree. I am very lucky for all this." Rebecca pushed her chin forward, determined not to remember, Sally guessed. How on earth could she bear it? And hide her horror most of the time with such a bright face?

* * *

There wasn't any shelter at the Simpkinses on the night their town had its first air-raid warning. Sally woke as soon as the soaring wail of the siren blew. She lay in terror listening to its melancholy rise and fall. She heard Clara and Sue turn and grumble, still asleep in their bed on the other side of the room. Should she wake them? Mum was there in the room the next moment and saved her from having to make that decision.

"Mum?" she asked in the dark.

"Oh good, you're awake. Help me with these two, will you? We're going under the stairs. Dad's taking Jim down."

You'd think Mum had been used to air raids all her life, she sounded so matter-of-fact. This made Sally determined not to show how scared she was as she went over to lift Sue out of bed. Both of her younger sisters were still stubbornly refusing to wake up. They were too heavy to be carried all the way downstairs, like Dad was carrying Jim, but every time Mum or Sally stood one of them up on her own she would groan and flop back onto the bed again.

"To think I complain because they're too lively," Mum laughed. "Come on, Clara, up you get. Please. You can go back to sleep when we're settled downstairs."

The siren stopped wailing, but they could hear another one farther away toward the center of town still warning the people there.

"Oh, *quick,*" Sally shrieked at Sue, who was trying to snuggle down at her feet. What if they were trapped up there when the bombs came? She pulled Sue up roughly, not caring if she hurt her, and was rewarded by Sue waking up enough to complain. She half dragged, half pushed her, and Mum did the same with Clara. Somehow they all reached the safety of downstairs. The week before, Mum and Dad had cleared away the usual muddle from under the stairs, putting most of it out for salvage, and the rest in the garden shed.

"Just in time, eh?" said Dad, as they squashed together in a row, sitting on the floor, backs to the wall, with Jim on Dad's lap.

Clara and Sue were wide awake now, as excited as though this were a surprise party. Their chatter eased Sally's fear, and stopped her from listening for the distant drone of aircraft.

"Will a bomb drop right here?" asked Sue.

"I don't expect so," said Mum. "They wouldn't want to waste any of their bombs on us."

"How long will it last?" asked Clara.

"Don't ask me. Hitler didn't send me a timetable," Dad answered.

"We'll all be stiff if we have to stay here much longer," Sue grumbled.

"Do exercises with your legs," suggested Sally. "Look, you can do it without kicking anyone. Start by wriggling your toes, now your feet, now your ankles. That's right. Now, bend your knees up."

"You're a good girl, Sally," Mum murmured in the spooky light from the electric bulb, painted dark blue because of wartime rules about lights near outside doors.

Time ticked by, and there was no noise from outside. One and a half hours after the warning siren had sounded, the sudden, steady note of the "All Clear" shrilled into the quiet night. This noise woke Jim, who joined in with his own high wail of fright. They had to spend the next few minutes quelling his fears.

"Right. Back to bed, quick sharp," said Mum.

Sally joined Clara and Sue in pleas to stay up longer. It seemed a waste to go to bed now, but Mum and Dad said they weren't having any nonsense.

"You've got school tomorrow."

"Not tomorrow. Today now," shouted Clara with glee.

"All the more reason to get to sleep right now."

To Sally's amazement she did just that. In no time at all it seemed Mum was calling her to get up or she'd be late for school.

"We've got our names down for a Morrison shelter," Dad told them a few days later.

"A Morrison? What's that?" they all wanted to know.

"Wait and see."

Everyone seemed to say that about new air-raid shelters, Sally thought, remembering how mysterious Rebecca had been about the transformation of the Trevelyans' cellar.

Two days later a van parked outside the front gate, and Dad, home from work, helped the driver unload four large sheets of thick wire mesh, held rigid by metal bands along their edges. Last of all was a rectangular piece of solid, thick metal, as wide and as long as a double bed.

"Here we are then. Our air-raid shelter."

"How can we fix it up? We haven't got a dugout yet," Sally said.

"Don't need a dugout," Dad said as he went past holding his end of the metal sheet. "It's an indoor shelter for us. Posh. Stay clear, kids."

Mum folded up their gate-legged table, and she and Sally moved it out of the dining room to the space under the stairs. Then Dad sent everyone out of the dining room while he set about putting the shelter together. This took about an hour, and a few swear words they weren't supposed to hear, but at last he called them in to admire their shelter.

A giant cage with mesh sides, it took up three-quarters of the room. Dad showed them how the mesh sides could be pulled out to make a table they could sit at with their legs under. "And from now on that's where you lot will sleep when there's a raid. There'll be plenty of room, I reckon."

"I hope there's a raid tonight," said Clara.

"Yeah, so do I," said Sue.

"Calm down, you two," Mum said. "And don't go wishing for things you might regret."

They had a trial run. The girls and Jim crawled in, with plenty of room to spare.

"Come on, Mum. You come and practice too," Clara called.

"Oh, all right, then. Shove over, make room for a little one."

If they all stretched out to sleep, there'd never be room for Dad.

"We'll worry about that when the time comes," he said.

And it wasn't many nights before they had to use it in a real raid. Mum had spread a couple of eiderdowns on the floor to make it more comfortable to lie on, and they had blankets to keep them warm. Lying there, with Dad sitting alongside in the easy chair by the side of the fireplace, they heard the first wave of planes droning overhead. They sounded ominous. Sally held her breath until she felt her face swelling. The planes flew over several at a time, half an hour between each group, disturbing her every time she started to fall asleep. It was impossible to tell whether the explosions she heard in the distance were bombs or anti-aircraft guns. The "All Clear" siren was lullaby music.

After that, there were raids almost every night, and they grew used to sleeping with the roar of planes overhead. Dad took his turn fire-watching once a fortnight. The German planes went on flying over their town on their way to bomb other places. It was almost peaceful—until they put the anti-aircraft gun at the bottom of their street.

One night, Sally was dozing, drifting into sleep, when a crash, louder than anything she'd ever heard, startled her awake. Jim screamed, and Clara and Sue whimpered. Sally lay rigid with terror, her head and ears ringing. It could only be a bomb. Dad had automatically dropped from his chair and lay flat on the floor. Amazingly the house stayed in one piece. They were all beginning to relax when there was a whoosh and another deafening explosion.

"By heck," said Dad, "that's not bombs. That's anti-aircraft shells. They must have put a gun down the street. I'll be jiggered."

"It'll be in the playing fields," said Mum. "Has to be, they surely wouldn't risk shooting one down over the houses, would they, Ken?"

"Why ask me? No, all right, I don't suppose they would."

The sky became quiet, and they were all asleep by the time the "All Clear" sounded.

The next day the fears of the night were forgotten because of the discovery, in their own front garden, of pieces of shrapnel from the shells. And, after that, Clara and Sue raced out every morning to go shrapnel hunting. Sally secretly envied them, as she'd have liked to do the same, but it didn't seem quite the right thing for a Lord George's girl.

10 ❖ Air Raids

A few nights later they had one of the longest raids so far, and they hadn't learned to sleep through the noise of the anti-aircraft gun, so nobody was feeling very bright at breakfast time. The ringing of the phone woke them more than the alarm clock had done, it was so unusual at that time of the day. And it was scary. Mum's face went white; she dropped her teaspoon into her saucer with a clink.

"It's Dad. I know it's him. We should have made him stay here, stubborn old . . ."

"Don't panic, Mabel. It could be anything. I'll take it, you stay here." Dad was out of the room already.

Everyone sat still, listening to Dad's voice, unable to understand any words. Mum, still white and trembly, got up from the table and went out, shutting the door firmly behind her. Jim turned his head from side to side, looking at his sisters between blinks and sniffs.

"Here, Jim, eat this." Sally pushed a long slice of toast into his mouth just as he opened it to let out the first yell. Jim chewed on this, while the rest of them sat waiting, scared by Mum's fear. They had never seen her like that before.

The sound of the door opening made them jump, although one look at Mum's face told them that the news wasn't as bad as she'd feared.

"Yes, it's Grandpa," Mum said.

"On the phone?" asked Sally.

"No," said Dad, "that was the hospital. Don't worry!" He laughed at their gasps. "They're not even keeping him in."

Mum took over. "We're going to have him here for a bit. His house caught it last night, but thank goodness he's only got a broken arm and a couple of broken ribs. These days they need every possible bed, so they've asked us to fetch him today. He'll be here when you get home from school."

"Goody, goody!" Clara and Sue bounced up and down on their chairs.

"And just remember, he's had a terrible shock, as well as his injuries. He'll not want you two dancing around him like mad dervishes. He's coming here for a bit of peace and quiet."

Clara and Sue put on faces of offended innocence.

"Is his house completely ruined?" Sally asked with concern.

"No idea," Dad answered. "We didn't speak to him, see. But I don't reckon it could be too bad for him to escape like that. Anyhow, this settles it. He's not going back there." He looked at the clock on the mantelpiece.

"Hey, take a look at the time, will you? You'll all be late for school if you don't get a move on."

"What about you and work, then? You should have left twenty minutes ago," Sally told him.

"No, I'll give them a ring, tell them I'll not be in today. We can't have your mum going over there to collect Grandpa on her own."

They left Mum and Dad making plans for the rescue. And when Sally came home from school later there was Grandpa, his arm in plaster, his body bulky from the strapping around his ribs.

"Grandpa!" She rushed over to hug him but stopped just in front of his chair. "Whoops! I'd better go easy on those broken bones, eh?" She bent down to kiss him gently, and he gripped her shoulder so hard she knew she'd have bruises there tomorrow.

Clara and Sue made obvious efforts to restrain their usual high spirits at teatime, subdued by Grandpa's quietness, but as they were helping to clear the table Clara turned to him.

"You haven't told us what it's like being bombed out. What happened?"

For a moment Grandpa looked exactly like Jim when he didn't know whether to cry or not. He turned to Mum for help.

"Grandpa doesn't want to talk about it today, Clara. Leave him alone now, there's a good girl. He's very tired."

And indeed he settled down on the settee bed in the front room as soon as tea was over.

"Just please God those rotten planes leave us alone tonight," said Mum when she left Grandpa, who was already drifting into a weary sleep.

Mum's plea must have been heard, for there was no raid that night.

Dad took the next day off work as well, to sort out what was left of Grandpa's belongings. The bomb-damage inspectors said that all parts of houses left standing in the row where he'd lived would have to come down. It was far too dangerous to try to repair any of the buildings. Of his furniture, his bed, wardrobe, and old armchair were saved—nothing else.

"I don't mind all the rest, only my dear old harmonium," he said, when they told him this. Sally was horrified, then terribly sad, to see tears roll down his cheeks. He didn't seem to notice. She thought of the hours he used to spend playing that harmonium, singing his favorite hymns.

That day Mum and Dad changed the living room into a bedroom for Grandpa. The only trouble was that there was hardly any space to walk around.

"We'll have to shift the furniture, I reckon," said Dad. "Leave the old boy his own bits and pieces."

"All in good time," Mum said.

It was one thing having Grandpa stay with them for holidays, thought Sally, but a very different kettle of fish having him for keeps. There just wasn't enough room, not with his furniture as well. He must have been thinking the same.

"It won't be for long," he said at teatime. "You've got enough on your hands, Mabel, without having to put up with me."

"Dad, don't talk so daft!"

"We want you to stay, Grandpa, really we do," Clara assured him. "Don't we?" she challenged the others.

"Yes, yes, of course," everyone said, and they all meant it, even Dad. And Grandpa was Mum's father, not his.

"All the same, it does mean more work and worry for Mum," Sally said the next day on her way to school with Rebecca.

"I can see it would."

And more squashing up for all of us, Sally added to herself. Not to mention one more waiting for the lavatory in the mornings. She felt guilty for thinking such thoughts, so she didn't say them out loud. But they were true, weren't they?

Sally was as surprised as everyone else when the phone rang that evening. Mrs. Trev wanted to speak to Mum.

"She wants me to go to see her tomorrow morning," said Mum in a puzzled voice when she'd hung up. "You haven't been up to anything, have you, our Sally?"

Sally tried to think of any possible crimes she and Rebecca might have committed lately, and was able to say no quite sincerely. She was as puzzled as Mum was.

"Maybe she wants you to go on one of her committees," said Dad. They all fell about laughing at the idea.

"I don't know what you think's so funny about that," said Mum. "Why shouldn't she want me on one of her committees? I might well surprise the lot of you one of these days."

The next day was Saturday, so Sally went along to give Mum support. Mum dressed carefully for the visit, and left instructions with Dad about getting dinner started if they weren't back by twelve.

"Don't bother so, Mum," said Sally. "She's nobody to

be scared of, honestly. She's just as ordinary as anyone else once you get used to her."

Mum didn't look convinced.

Celia Trevelyan opened the front door as they walked up the path, and reached forward to Sally to give her the brushing kiss on her cheek that was their normal greeting now.

"Hello, Mrs. Trev," said Sally. If Mum was startled by this casual familiarity she hid it well. "This is my mother. Mum, this is Mrs. Trevelyan."

In the living room they sat side by side on the golden velvet settee, Mum right on its edge, as if she were scared her bottom might be too common for such richness. Rebecca came into the room and sat on one of the golden chairs. She gave Mrs. Trev a conspiratorial smile.

"Mrs. Simpkins," Mrs. Trev began, "I hope you won't take what I'm going to say amiss, or think that I'm interfering in any way."

She talked for several minutes about the problems of wartime living, disruption of families, people having to adapt to new situations. Finally, she worked around to suggesting that Grandpa move into the Trevelyan household.

Mum and Sally sat in amazed silence. The thought of Grandpa living in the grand Trevelyan house was truly staggering.

"Of course you can't be expected to answer straight away," Mrs. Trev concluded, "and I most certainly don't want to rob you of his company, but it seems so practical when we have so much room to spare and, well, frankly, there are a lot of you, aren't there? It's up to you and your father, of course, but the offer's there. If he agrees he'd have his own quarters, naturally, and we wouldn't interfere with his comings and goings. I'm sorry, I'm afraid I don't know his name.''

"Mr. Baker," said Mum in a weak voice, "Daniel Baker. My word, this really does take some thinking about. I don't know what to say. It's very kind of you, Mrs. Trevelyan . . .''

"Oh, my dear, don't think of it like that. I'm not suggesting this out of charity, believe me. As a matter of fact, you'll be doing us a good turn if you agree. If we don't take in your father we'll probably have some unbelievably ghastly family foisted on us anyway. Anyone with a room or two to spare has to be prepared for that sort of thing these days, I'm afraid. But I'm sure Sally's grandfather would fit in very well. And of course he'd pay us rent, enough to cover expenses.''

She smiled serenely at them, while Sally had a hard time not to scream at her. Mrs. Trev was every bit as bad as Mum and Dad had hinted, just another snob, despite all she'd done for Rebecca. Sally's face grew hot with confusion.

A few minutes later they all stood up, and Mrs. Trev turned to Sally. "We'll see you some time over the weekend, won't we?" She looked at Mum. "We're all so very fond of Sally, you know, Mrs. Simpkins. You must be proud of her.''

Well, maybe she wasn't so bad after all. Sally couldn't keep back a smile when she saw Mum's astonished face.

All the way home they talked about the suggestion. "It really would be a good idea, Mum. It's close enough for us to visit any time, and for him to come and see us whenever he feels like it.''

"But the Trevelyans. I'm not saying they're stuck up or anything, but he'd be like a fish out of water. He wouldn't know how to talk to them."

"Grandpa? He could talk to the king if he had to."

At that, Mum laughed and had to agree. "I must admit it would be a load off my mind to know he was in a proper shelter when there was a raid."

"Well, that beats the band. I'll have to think it over, won't I?" said Grandpa when they told him about it. "Say I went, and I'm not making any promises, understand, but just say I did go, do you reckon they'd let me take my own furniture? What's left of it."

"I daresay they would, can't see any reason why not, can you, Sally?"

"No, they've got loads of room. Anyway, there's no harm in asking."

There followed a weekend of phone calls, and on Monday morning, Paul Trevelyan sent one of his factory vans to pick up Grandpa's belongings. After school that afternoon, Mum and Sally walked with Grandpa to his new home. He strode along briskly, the dazzling white of his plaster matched by his hair and moustache.

The Trevelyans had made a room for him in the cellar. Mrs. Trev had hung a curtain across one part of the middle space to give him privacy, and she'd put an old rug on the raffia matting. Paul and she had fitted his bed, wardrobe, and armchair into this space, and had added a small table and a dining chair. Sally remembered it as one of the odd ones that used to be in the kitchen. Mrs. Trev told him that the bathroom down there was now his, except during air raids, when they'd all have to use it if necessary.

"By gum, it looks like home already, doesn't it, Mabel?" He turned his head away and sniffed rather noisily.

"I'll leave you to yourselves," said Mrs. Trev. "Just come up when you're ready."

Mum and Grandpa were both inclined to be weepy as they sorted out his clothes, but Sally couldn't help feeling excited about the whole idea. They brightened up, too, before they went back up the cellar steps to make final arrangements with Mrs. Trev.

"Don't feel you have to shut yourself away down there all day," she told Grandpa. "The garden's there for all of us all the time."

"You're not planning to turn me into a troglodyte, then?"

Mrs. Trev's eyes widened at the surprising word. "Certainly not." She smiled as she poured cups of tea. "I have a feeling it's going to be fun having you here," she said as she carefully put Grandpa's cup on the side table next to his good arm.

11 ❖ Grandpa's Place

"All right, Hitler, you can give us a breathing space,"
Mum grumbled. They'd only been back a couple of hours
after seeing Grandpa settled in, and there went the siren.
Just as the little ones were fast asleep, too. Sally helped
carry them down to the Morrison, and wriggled in after
them. Dad went off fire-watching.

Sally lay on her side, her back to Clara, with Sue's head
at the other end of the shelter, her feet stretched out to
Sally's back. Mum and Jim were on the other side of Clara.
They'd all put on their pajamas and settled down for the
night. Once there was a raid on, you got what sleep you
could. Sally stared through the mesh into the room lit by
the dying fire, the coals glowing brightly in the dark.

The shattering clang of the anti-aircraft gun woke her
and made her head ring, as always.

"That was a good one," said Mum, and Sue's scared
whimper changed to a laugh. Jim groaned but stayed asleep.

Another whoosh and clang startled them again.

"I'm coming up your end," said Sue. She turned around and wriggled up until her head was level with Sally's and Clara's. They lay snuggled together like a litter of kittens.

The next explosion was different, no whoosh of the shell flying upward. The crash itself was not so clangy; it was more like a very, very loud thud. For half a minute there was absolute silence, then a dull, soft roar, the whole house shaking as though there was an earthquake. From the front came a steady tinkle, tinkle of gently breaking glass, sounding orderly, not at all violent.

"That was a bomb," Sally said.

"Just keep still," Mum commanded, and they all lay back. It was eerily quiet, the drone of the planes fading as they moved on to further destruction.

"Someone should go and see if everything's all right in the front," said Sally after a few minutes. "That glass was in the house."

"All the more reason for not going in there now. Wait till morning," Mum said. "If the windows have gone, the blackout shades will be torn and useless at hiding the light . . ." She was interrupted by the sound of the door opening.

"Don't panic," Dad's voice called from the hallway, "it's only me. Just came to make sure everyone was still in one piece."

He opened the dining room door and put on the light. One look at him and the whole family burst out laughing.

"Ken, what a sight! You're not hurt, are you?"

"No, I'm right as rain, thanks to the mud patch up the street. Now you can see why we always hang around there. Better a bit of mud than broken bones." The whole of his front, including his face, was sticky and dark. "Look, I can't stay long, got to go back on duty. I just came around to make sure you were all right. Keep out of the front rooms, upstairs as well. You'll have to stay here the rest of the night, even after the 'All Clear' has gone."

"Have our bedroom windows broken too?" asked Clara.

"Not a pane left anywhere in the front."

"Gosh." There was stunned, excited silence.

"I'd better go and get cleaned up a bit, then I'll have to go back. Can't leave it all to the others."

"You've got time for a cuppa, surely." Mum had crawled out of the shelter as soon as he walked in, to go into the kitchen to put the kettle on.

"Oh, all right, then, but it'll have to be quick."

He went out and came back a little later with the worst of the mud washed off. By now they'd all scrambled out of the shelter and were eager to hear about the bomb. None of the houses on the street had any serious damage. A few, like theirs, had windows blown out.

"Funny the way a bomb blast goes. Numbers one and three have got some of their windows out, five and seven haven't got a crack, as far as we can see. And here we are, at number nine, the worst off of the lot."

It made them feel important.

"So nobody's been hurt?" asked Sally.

Dad took a slurp of tea. "Afraid I can't say that. The gun crew copped it; the bomb landed right next to them. Must have been what the Germans were aiming at."

"What happened to the men?" Mum asked.

"One of them's had it, killed outright, and the other two are in a bad way. The ambulance is on its way now." His face changed color as he said it. He drank the rest of his tea in one gulp. "Thanks, Mabel." He gave Mum a hug, and waved the girls toward the Morrison. "Go on, back inside, the lot of you. And stay there. Right?"

"Right, Dad."

They were settling down when Sally had a new thought. "Hey," she said aloud. "What if Grandpa had still been here? He'd have been in that front room."

"It doesn't bear thinking about," said Mum. "All that flying glass."

"We got him out just in the nick of time, didn't we?" said Sally. "A sort of miracle."

Grandpa soon settled down in his new home, as Sally had guessed he would, after that first conversation he'd had with Mrs. Trev.

"But you can't feed yourself properly, with only that oil stove to cook on, Dad," Mum had argued.

"Oh, can't I just?" he'd replied. "You wait and see. It'll do me champion. What more do I need, with the rationing? I'm not going to be roasting any joints of meat, am I? Remember, I'm used to looking after myself, and this suits me just fine."

It certainly seemed to. Sally went to visit him on Thursday afternoon, when she had a half-day holiday at Lord George's, and he looked as chirpy as she'd ever seen him, despite the plastered arm. His face was round and rosy again, his blue eyes were sparkler-bright.

"They've given me another room of my own, too. Upstairs. Come on, I'll show you."

He led her up the cellar steps and around outside to the side of the house. There they stopped in a paved courtyard, sheltered by a brick wall with a pear tree growing against it. Grandpa felt in his pocket, and brought out a large iron key.

"Shall I do that for you?"

"No need, lass, thanks all the same. I can manage perfectly well on my own." And he set about proving his independence.

He unlocked the glass-paned door, in a glass-paned wall, and they walked into a narrow, long room, curtained and locked off from the rest of the house. Grandpa explained that it used to be a conservatory, later used by the Trevelyans for storing garden furniture. They'd cleared most of that to an outside shed, and left him a couple of chairs, a cane settee, and a small table.

"See, Mrs. Trev's put this rug in here, too. And these cushions make the chairs as comfy as anything you could wish for."

"Mrs. Trev, eh?" Sally laughed. "Didn't waste any time, did you?"

"Yes, well you call her that, don't you? And the young lass, your pal Rebecca, said she'd like it, so that's not taking any liberties, is it?"

"I suppose not. Gosh, Grandpa, it's good having you here." She wanted to give him a hug, but he waved his plastered arm at her.

"Careful of my ribs, lass. They're not right yet, you know. Not by a long chalk."

"Just a gentle one, then."

"See, you'll be able to visit me without disturbing anyone else. My own private entrance." He tapped the glass door. "They've given me the only key, so it's my responsibility to lock up here every night. But come on, I'll show you the way out."

Sally stopped herself from telling him that she knew this garden as well as her own. They stepped out together, walked along the side of the house toward the front garden, and strolled across the diagonal path that led to the main driveway.

"It's a grand place, this, isn't it?"

By the way he said it, Sally knew he didn't mean posh, but somewhere he could be really happy.

"Grand," she agreed, and hugged his good arm. They walked on for a few minutes in contented silence.

"Think I'd better have a bit of a nap," said Grandpa. "I'm feeling rather tired, all of a sudden."

"You're probably still suffering from shock."

"Maybe. And I'm not as young as I was."

"All right. You go and have a rest, and I'll go up to Rebecca. I'll come and see you before I leave. Say about four o'clock. How would that suit you?"

"That'll be grand, lass."

12 ❖ Rebecca Speaks Out

In Rebecca's room they experimented with hairstyles, combing and pinning, tying back and brushing forward, viewing the effects from all angles.

"You're lucky to have natural curls," said Sally. "I've asked Mum if I can have a perm, but she says I've got to wait till I'm fifteen. *Fifteen!*"

"Don't worry, you should keep it straight. It suits you. Here, try it like this." Rebecca combed Sally's hair back and up behind her ears, and clipped it into place. "Look at the way it shows off your cheekbones," she said. Sally just had time to admire this before one hair clip started slithering out and the hair flopped down again.

"See what I mean?" she wailed. "Who'd have mousey, thin, straight hair like mine?"

"At least you've got no spots," said Rebecca. She put her face close to the mirror and squeezed a blackhead on her chin. "Ouch," she said, as tears came to her eyes.

"Neither have you." Sally laughed. "Only that teensy one you need a microscope to see."

"Your grandpa's ever so nice, isn't he?" Rebecca moved away from the dressing table and lay back on her bed, hands beneath her head.

"Yes." Sally flopped onto the other end of the bed, on her tummy, and dug her elbows into the eiderdown, her chin propped up by her fists.

"I never knew my grandfathers, either of them." Rebecca had closed her eyes, and was talking in a dreamy voice.

"Did they die before you were born?" Sally kept her voice quiet, too, but made it as ordinary and matter-of-fact as she could.

"No, Mami's father was still alive, but he and my grandmother lived in Holland, so we never saw them. They were Dutch. So I'm partly Dutch. Jewish Dutch and Jewish German. Maybe now they are dead as well. I think Mami and Papi are, and Helmut. I think by now the Nazis will have killed them all. It's no use to hope for a miracle."

Sally felt there was nothing she could say to comfort her friend. She knew that Rebecca didn't want words from her, only her being there, to listen and try to understand.

But real understanding was beyond her imagination. If she tried hard she could imagine what it might be like to be an orphan, and to have an only brother killed too. What Rebecca had to live with must be a thousand times worse. She didn't know for certain if her mother and father and brother were alive or dead, or if they were being held by the Gestapo.

Sally remembered with shame the times she'd envied Rebecca the luxury she lived in. Had envied her for petty things like being able to play tennis in games, instead of softball, because she had her own racket and had already had lessons. She'd envied her for having her own bathroom when she, Sally, was standing shivering and nearly bursting, waiting to use their one and only lavatory in the mornings.

Rebecca was muttering words Sally couldn't quite hear, and she realized they weren't English; they must be German or Yiddish. This went on for several minutes. Suddenly she gave a gasp and was silent.

"I'm sorry, Sally," she said clearly a moment later. "I think I was dreaming." Her eyes opened, and she looked at the foot of the bed where Sally still lay with her chin on her hands.

"I think you were. Are you all right?"

"Yes, thanks." She rubbed her hands across her face, drying away her tears. "How strange to go off like that. I'm sorry."

"Don't be sorry, it's all right. Must be in the air. Grandpa's having a nap too."

"Yes, your grandpa. That was when I fell asleep, when we talked about grandfathers, wasn't it? Was I asleep long?"

"Only a few minutes. Honestly. But it wouldn't have mattered if it had been hours, would it? Don't look so worried. You obviously needed the rest just like Grandpa did after our walk around the garden."

"But he's an old man of seventy or more and I'll not be thirteen until next month."

"So what? You had a different reason for dozing off. You were remembering." Sally turned over, sat up, crossed her legs, and looked straight at Rebecca. "I've had an idea," she said. "I think you and Grandpa should adopt each other."

"What do you mean?" Rebecca sat up and stared back at Sally.

"Oh, nothing. Forget it."

"No, you can't say that now. Adopt? That's when a woman can't have her own baby, isn't it? I don't understand what you mean."

"I said forget it. I didn't mean adopt like that."

Rebecca shrugged. "If you say I must. But if not like that, like what?" She was mumbling, so that Sally had to strain to hear the last words. Then her voice went back to normal. "Let's try to do our maths homework, eh? I hate geometry, so let's get it over with."

This kept them busy for the next three-quarters of an hour. Sally looked up at the clock on the bookcase.

"Four o'clock. Perfect timing. I told Grandpa I'd go down and see him then. Come on."

He was in the sun room, wide awake after his afternoon sleep. Sally and Rebecca sat on each side of him on the cane settee.

"I suppose you've been putting the world to rights up there, have you?"

"No, Grandpa, we've been doing our maths homework."

"Yes, Mr. Baker, we've been very virtuous."

"Mr. Baker, Mr. Baker. It's about time you found something a bit easier to call me, isn't it? How about Daniel?"

"It doesn't sound right," said Rebecca. "I know I call Celia and Paul by their first names, but—"

"Why not call him 'Grandpa'?" said Sally. "People often say that to older people, even when they're not related."

"Yes. Grandpa!" Rebecca and he looked at each other and smiled their agreement. Sally smiled even more widely to herself. Now at last Rebecca had a grandpa. They'd adopted each other, whether they knew it or not.

"I've been thinking about Sunday," Grandpa said next. "I'd like to go to the Baptist chapel. I could walk it from here, couldn't I?"

"Easy. Remember we did it at Christmas?"

He nodded.

"Well, it's much nearer from here."

"Good, then. I'm going to find it a bit strange getting used to a new congregation, but the sooner the better." He blinked and wiped his fingers across his moustache. "I shouldn't complain, should I? Lucky to be alive."

"Gosh, Grandpa, don't talk about it. You'll be able to join the choir too. I bet they're short of basses."

"Just as long as they don't think I'm too old."

"Too old!" Sally laughed. "How could they? Especially with a voice like yours."

He ducked his head, but couldn't hide his delighted smile at the compliment. Sally smiled, too, remembering that Christmas morning service.

"I might go along with you," she said, amazing herself. She'd certainly not been thinking of anything like that a minute ago.

"That'd be grand, lass. You could show me the way in case I've forgotten."

"Fine. But right now I'd better be on my way home," she said to Grandpa and Rebecca. "Mum'll be expecting me."

"I'll see you to the gate," Grandpa told her, holding out his plastered arm in an old-fashioned gesture of Victorian manners. She laughed and rested her hand lightly on his arms, parodying a prim nineteenth-century miss.

"You come along, Rebecca, as well," Grandpa ordered. "I'll need a young lady to escort me back when I've seen this one on her way."

"Certainly, *Grandpa*," said Rebecca, laughing with him, her greenish blue eyes flashing brightly.

Together the three of them walked down the curved garden path. Sally, Grandpa, and Rebecca.

The war became background, taken for granted, and the air raids stopped. At school nobody thought of Rebecca as different anymore, until one day in English. Their Shakespeare play that term was *The Merchant of Venice*, and, as usual, they'd had to read it themselves as holiday homework. In the first English class of the new term, Miss Walker, the English teacher, was giving them a quick rundown of the story. They were doodling in their notebooks, gazing out of the windows or up at the ceiling, and even, in a few virtuous cases, listening to Miss Walker.

"I'm sure you've all studied the text with your usual diligence, and this term we'll—"

"*No!*"

The sudden exclamation startled all the girls into attention and Miss Walker into a moment's shocked silence.

". . . this term we'll be studying . . ." she continued, ignoring the interruption.

"No! I refuse to study this play. It's wicked."

"Rebecca Muller, how dare you be so impertinent!" But Miss Walker's voice had lost its usual confidence. She was obviously as amazed as the girls were by Rebecca's sudden outburst.

"I don't care if you think I'm impertinent."

You could have heard a pin drop. Rebecca Muller, of all people!

"This is a wicked play. Yes, wicked. Your wonderful Shakespeare was just another Jew hater. Why do you all hate us?" Rebecca stood up, furious.

Now the silence became embarrassing. Miss Walker recovered first. "Rebecca, that's simply not true. Look at what Shakespeare makes Shylock say: 'If you prick us, do we not bleed?' That's one of the best-known speeches in the play, and we'll be studying it as part of this term's course. So sit down, and calm down, Rebecca."

"I'm sorry, Miss Walker, but I can't. All right, that's one speech, and it's the only time he lets Shylock have his say. All the rest of the time everyone sneers at him, don't they?"

There was a shuffling of feet as boredom edged into the general feeling of discomfort. Who cared that much about just another term's Shakespeare? But Rebecca hadn't finished. And Miss Walker was letting her have her say.

"Look at Shylock's daughter, Jessica. She's a Jew and Shakespeare has to twist around so the only way the rest of them can accept her is because she becomes a Christian. It's horrible. Disgusting. Can't you see that?"

Rebecca sat down, slumped into her seat.

"Thank you, Rebecca," said Miss Walker. "Now girls, turn to page eighty-two in your grammar exercise books. Get to work."

Sally couldn't concentrate. Rebecca's reaction had punched into her memory. That day in elementary school when Rebecca had surprised all the class by singing "Silent Night," because she recognized the tune. And later, in the park, the day Rebecca talked about escaping from the Nazis.

"In Germany now to be Jewish is to be bad people."

Sally heard again Rebecca's words, heard her voice. No wonder she was so hurt by *The Merchant of Venice*. But the whole class studied that play with more thought than they'd given to any of their other English literature books. Sally guessed that Rebecca had made even Miss Walker see it afresh.

13 ❖ Victoria Station

1945. The Allied armies, forces of liberation, were advancing through Occupied Europe. After almost six years, the war was moving to its inevitable end. The Allies reached Germany and went on marching. Rumors began to circulate, rumors about the discovery of unimaginable horrors. One morning stories and photographs were released, published in newspapers, and the name Belsen hit a stunned world. What had happened was far worse than the worst of the rumors—it was horrible beyond belief—but it was all true.

Sally was seventeen and had left school almost a year ago to start her nurse's training. In the hospital where she worked she had seen some gruesome injuries and had helped to care for very sick and dying patients, although in her junior role all she was allowed to do was help to make their beds and empty their bedpans. None of the sights she'd seen could have prepared her for the shock of those first concentration camp photographs.

"It's so unbelievably hideous that human beings could do that to other human beings," she said to Mum and Dad as they sat at breakfast, the newspaper lying open between them, next to the bread and margarine that suddenly none of them could eat. "It's much worse than all the straight killings with bombs, isn't it? How *could* they? Oh, my God, I feel sick."

She rushed out to the bathroom and bent over the lavatory bowl, retching, having nothing to vomit from her empty stomach.

Rebecca. Rebecca must be going through hell, reading those stories, seeing the photographs of those living skeletons who had survived Belsen. Men and women hardly recognizable as people, their eyes stark and staring, dreadfully alive, in bodies that were almost dead. She must be wondering if any of those emaciated people were her family—her parents, her brother.

Rebecca still went to school. She'd be going to university if she did well enough in her final school exams, and nobody doubted that she would. They were still close friends, although their lives were now so different, but there was no chance of them getting together until Sally was off duty at seven o'clock. She didn't have a date that evening, and she'd have broken it if she had, if Rebecca wanted to see her. Rebecca only went out with boys on weekends, because of all the studying she had to do, a rule she'd made herself. So if she wanted to talk, or if she just wanted them to be together . . .

"No," said Rebecca on the phone. "Thanks very much,

but I'm going to immerse myself in Latin tonight, so that I won't be able to think. Know what I mean?"

"Of course."

At Lord George's they hadn't been taught Latin, but to enter a university in the 1940s Rebecca had to pass Latin at tenth grade level. So she and the other students who wanted to go to a university had a crash course, which they had to fit around the rest of their intensive studies. There were times when Sally was glad that she'd gone into nursing, and left school after the tenth year.

VE Day, May 8, 1945. Everyone in England seemed to go mad, because the war in Europe was over. That day it was impossible for Rebecca to shut out memories of her German childhood, the happy times with her parents and brother, and the nightmare months before Celia had rescued her, but Mami, Papi, and Helmut had stayed behind. Guilt swept over her, as it had so often during the last seven years—guilt because she dared to be so happy, forgetting her family for minutes, sometimes hours at a time. Rationally, she knew that this was right, that her suffering wouldn't help them, if indeed they were still alive to be helped. Emotionally, this logic seemed wrong.

What had happened to them? Please let them have died quickly, she silently prayed to a God she didn't believe in but appealed to all the same.

How would she find out what had happened to them? Celia was the perfect person to investigate, and in fact she and her helpers were already working, trying to trace the families of the refugees they had rescued before the war, including Rebecca's family, the Mullers.

One day early in July Celia called to her as she came in from school.

"I have news," she told her. "And there's no possibility of error; I've waited until it was all checked and double-checked before saying anything to you. It's good and bad."

Get on with it, Rebecca wanted to scream, but she managed to keep quiet.

"Your parents are both dead; they died early in the war, in the Auschwitz gas chambers."

Rebecca felt cold, although it was a warm day. She began to shake violently, uncontrollably, willing Celia not to move toward her. Physical sympathy would have broken her down to tears, wailing. She sat shaking and speechless.

"There's more," Celia said after a few minutes' silence. "Helmut is alive. He was in Belsen, and he's now in a rehabilitation camp. He'll be coming to England as soon as the doctors think he's strong enough. His travel permit was easy to arrange because you're here."

"No! No! It's all wrong," Rebecca cried. "It's Mami and Papi who were supposed to be safe." She'd had secret dreams of them being hidden all through the war. For Helmut, she'd had no hopes or secret dreams. She'd been in Germany when the Gestapo had taken him away. And yet he'd somehow survived. She couldn't take it in. "It's all wrong," she said again.

Two weeks later Celia and Rebecca waited at Victoria Station for the train that carried the passengers from the boats at Dover. They'd traveled there by train. Even Celia couldn't wangle extra petrol coupons to allow them to drive all the way down to London.

Waiting at the barrier, Rebecca panicked. "I won't recognize him," she said.

"It doesn't matter. He'll have his identification papers. And he's expecting to see us." Celia's voice was firm, but for once it wasn't reassuring.

Because he was seven years older than Rebecca he'd been a remote figure in her childhood, not much more than a big brother to boast about at school. And during the war, she'd tried not to think about him. It was easier to imagine him dead than being tortured. How would anyone be who'd survived one of the death camps? After seven years would he come out the same as he'd gone in? Of course not. The rehabilitation doctors had let him go, but would he be sane, could anyone be sane after the starvation, the torture? She wanted to run away, to not have to face a wrecked Helmut.

The train drew into the station, carriage doors opened, people jumped or stepped cautiously onto the platform. They surged toward the barrier, passing through in a jostling mass. The crowd gradually thinned and suddenly Rebecca saw him. He wasn't the only solitary young man, nor the only thin one in ill-fitting clothes; he wasn't the only person hesitating, looking lost; Belsen had worn away any familiarity he might once have had. But Rebecca knew him, recognized him with absolute certainty, not from his appearance, but simply because she knew in her bones this was her brother.

"Helmut!" she called.

He looked her way, and the scowl on his face lifted for a moment. "Rebecca?"

"Yes, yes!"

He still had to go through the ticket barrier. Goodness

knew what problems they would face in the future, how scarred he was from the suffering he had endured through his young manhood. Terrible as this must have been, here he was now, her own brother, and she, with Celia and Paul, was here to help him, as much as anyone could, at the end of the nightmare.

❖ Epilogue: Australia Today

It was the last day of Clarissa's holiday at Nan and Grandpa's place at Ulladulla. She had an exercise book full of Nan's story, of her childhood and Rebecca's, in England during the war. But hardly a word about Grandpa. Typical. Grandpa never talked—he only sat fishing, and throwing back most of the fish he caught.

Clarissa needed Grandpa to talk to her if she was going to make this the greatest school project ever. How could she get him going?

Suddenly she remembered a scene from her own younger days and she knew that Grandpa would never talk about his wartime experiences. Why had she been so stupid? Why hadn't she remembered his sudden recoil when she was four or five, when she had said, "Why have you got those numbers on your arm, Grandpa?"

She'd been fascinated by the blue blurry tattoo, just having learned what written numbers looked like. Mum and

Dad had both grabbed her and pulled her away with rough hands. It was a dim horror memory and she couldn't recall anything Grandpa had said. Where had he gone for the rest of the day?

After that she'd never seen the sinister tattooed numbers on his forearm again. Grandpa always wore long-sleeved shirts, even on the hottest days, and he never rolled back his sleeves.

Clarissa sat quietly beside Grandpa all the rest of that last holiday afternoon. She swung her legs idly over the stone wall where he hung out his fishing line. She'd been scared of him as long as she could remember, not knowing why, because he was always gentle. The sudden vivid memory had taken away all his scariness. Now she was scared for him, not scared of him. No. Sorry for him. Feeling for him. Knowing she couldn't help him. Except by loving him, as only a granddaughter could.

Great-aunt Rebecca had stayed in England, and become an important professor there. Clarissa remembered seeing her only once on a visit to Australia, when she, Clarissa, was a young child. Maybe she could ask Nan why she and Grandpa had come out here so soon after they were married in England, a few years after the war ended. She'd ask to see their faded, old-fashioned black and white wedding photos again. There were only two: one with all those great-aunts, and one of just the bride and groom, Sally and Helmut Muller.

❖ About the Author

MARY BAYLIS-WHITE writes from firsthand experience about growing up in England under the cloud of war: "The events in *Sheltering Rebecca* are history today, but a lot of memory for me."

Mary Baylis-White is the author of several books for young readers. She makes her home in Sydney, Australia.